Deadly Pursuit

Nate concentrated on the task at hand, threading among the trees with the same skill as his Indian companions. He saw Buffalo Horn look back at him two or three times.

As the chase continued, the Flatheads were goaded on by the distant whoops of their fierce mortal enemies. When the forest gave way to a series of hills, Running Elk took the lead in winding among them.

Looking over his shoulder, Nate was startled to find four of the Utes had pulled out well ahead of the rest and were closing the gap rapidly.

Running Elk skirted a hill and, hemmed in on both sides by high rock walls, entered a ravine. The rest promptly followed.

Nate didn't like being boxed in. Should the Utes gain the rim, the Flatheads would be easy to pick off. So, for that matter, would Shakespeare and he. Nate avoided a boulder in his path and saw Running Elk bear to the right as the ravine curved. Seconds later he galloped around the turn and was stunned to discover the Flatheads bunched together at the base of another stone wall.

The ravine was a dead end.

The *Wilderness* series
published by Leisure Books:

7

WILDERNESS

Vengeance Trail

David Thompson

LEISURE BOOKS   NEW YORK CITY

Dedicated to
Judy, Joshua and Shane

A Leisure Book ®

October 1991

Published by

Dorchester Publishing Co., Inc.
276 Fifth Avenue
New York, NY 10001

Chapter One

The lone rider reined up on the crest of a rise and surveyed the pristine landscape below. He was a tall, muscular man, not yet twenty years of age, as hard as iron and radiating vitality. Buckskins and moccasins clothed his powerful frame. On his head perched a brown beaver hat. Jutting from under the hat, at the rear, was the tip of a white eagle feather securely tied to his shoulder-length black hair. His green eyes noted every detail of the terrain with delight.

A February thaw had transformed the Rocky Mountains from a snow shrouded wilderness into a prematurely glorious, spring-like wonderland. Temperatures in the fifties and sixties over the past week and a half had melted most of the white mantle, causing the rivers and streams to run full and tinged the brown grass with a dash of green. A few deciduous trees, fooled by the unseasonal warmth, had started to bud. The perennial evergreens, smarter and hardier, had only to lose their heavy, hoary blankets of wet, packed flakes to present the illusion of springtime.

Nodding in satisfaction, the young man urged his big black stallion down the slope. Had anyone been watching, they would have noticed that he appeared armed as if for a war. Slanted across his chest were a powder horn and a bullet pouch. Two flintlocks were nestled under his wide brown leather belt, one on each side of the buckle. A butcher knife with a 12-inch blade rested in a beaded sheath on his right hip. Angled under his belt above his left hip was a tomahawk. And resting across his thighs, his left hand loosely holding it in place, was a Hawken rifle. A Mackinaw coat and a bedroll were positioned snugly behind the saddle, and dangling from the saddle horn was a water bag.

He picked his way with care down the slippery slope and breathed a sigh of relief when he reached the valley floor below. Scanning the land ahead, he searched for any sign of smoke that might be drifting skyward from the cabin he'd traveled twenty-five miles to reach. The azure heavens, however, were crystal clear.

Cradling the Hawken in the crook of his left elbow, he pressed onward. Although he saw no hint of habitation, he felt certain he was in the right valley. His best friend and mentor, Shakespeare McNair, lived in this remote nook of the world near the top of the Rockies. He was eager to find the grizzled mountaineer and ask his advice on two important matters.

A gurgling stream bisected the valley and he took the west bank, riding northward, seeing wildlife or signs of wildlife everywhere. Sparrows and chickadees chirped and frolicked in the undergrowth. Ravens and jays occupied the tall trees. Rabbits bounded from his path. Once he flushed an elk, and twice he saw black-tailed deer in the distance. Along the stream, imprinted in the dark soil, were the tracks of countless creatures that had quenched their thirst at the water's edge. There were tiny chipmunk tracks and huge bear tracks, panther tracks and bobcat tracks, wolf tracks and fox tracks. He saw them all as he traveled a half-mile, and then he saw the cabin.

He almost missed it, so cleverly was the log structure blended into the surrounding forest. Shakespeare had constructed it at the base of a knoll fifty yards from the stream. Enormous pines ringed it, affording shade and protection from the elements. There was a pen for horses on the north side and a small shed to the south. A narrow strip of ground near the front door had been cleared of all brush, but otherwise the undergrowth was undisturbed. It was as if Shakespeare had deliberately built the cabin so it wouldn't disrupt the natural flow of things, just like an Indian would do.

Turning the stallion, he rode toward his friend's home. He noticed that no smoke curled from the sturdy stone chimney. Either Shakespeare wasn't in, he reasoned, or the grizzled mountaineer was forgoing a fire because of the warm weather. Suddenly he realized the front door was hanging open several inches and his eyes narrowed suspiciously.

Shakespeare would never go off and leave the door open knowing that a wandering bear or some other critter might waltz on in and help itself to the food supply and whatever else appeared tasty. He approached the cabin cautiously. Nothing stirred inside or out.

When the stallion was only ten feet from the door, he stopped. Gripping the Hawken in both hands, he slid to the ground and cocked the hammer. The loud click made him frown. Anyone or anything inside was bound to have heard it.

He advanced quickly and moved to the left of the

doorway, leaning against the jamb so he could peer within. The sight he beheld chilled the blood in his veins.

The interior of the cabin was in a shambles. Furniture had been upended, personal effects strewn about, and various items smashed to bits. Clothing lay in disarray. Broken dishes littered one corner.

Stark fear coursed through the young man's body. All he could think of was that his mentor had been slain, and in his mind's eye he envisioned Shakespeare being tomahawked or scalped. His heart beat wildly and his temples pounded. For a moment he felt dizzy. "Get a grip on yourself, Nate King," he said sternly.

Somewhere nearby a bird chirped.

The innocent sound served to snap Nate out of his anxious daze. He shook his head to clear his thoughts and stepped inside. Relief flared when he realized his friend's body was nowhere in the cabin. Perhaps, he told himself hopefully, Shakespeare was still alive. But if so, who had done this to the cabin and where was McNair?

He pivoted, scouring the room. Abruptly, he spied the large book lying on the floor next to an overturned table and stepped over to it. The title was easily discernible, and he read it with acute trepidation: THE COMPLETE WORKS OF WILLIAM SHAKE-SPEARE.

Nate's stomach muscles constricted. His friend would never go anywhere without that book. The volume had been Shakespeare's pride and joy, his constant companion on the trail or at home, going wherever he went to be read at any hour of the day or night. It was part of the reason McNair had long ago acquired the nickname 'Shakespeare'; that, and the fact McNair could quote countless passages from memory and did so with a striking eloquence.

If the book was there, Nate concluded, then his friend must be dead. He picked up the volume, righted the table, and gently placed the heavy book on top. Next he searched the cabin for traces of blood but found none. Mystified, he went outdoors and halted in consternation.

There were signs of Indians all over the place, clearly marked in the spongy soil. If not for the melted snow, the ground would have been too hard to bear many prints. He examined them at length and concluded the Indians had visited the cabin within the previous twenty-four hours and departed within the past twelve.

Chiding himself for not noticing the signs before, Nate bent at the waist and did the best he could reading the tracks. He wasn't as skilled as his mentor —yet—but he knew enough to deduce that ten mounted warriors had ridden up and eleven men had departed. He saw footprints he felt certain had been made by Shakespeare, leading to the inescapable conclusion that his friend had ridden off with the warriors.

Or been forced to accompany them.

Why else was the cabin a shambles? Nate mused. He turned, more perplexed now than ever. If hostile Indians had been responsible, they would have burned the building to the ground. Then again, while some of Shakespeare's things had been broken, most were undamaged. The clothes weren't torn to ribbons and the furniture was still intact. Hostiles would have taken particular delight in totally destroying both.

Nate let the hammer down on his rifle and thoughtfully scratched his chin. This made no sense, he noted. Friendly Indians wouldn't have committed such an outrage and hostiles would have skinned Shakespeare alive on the spot.

Strange.

He began executing a wide circle around the dwelling, seeking more signs. The trail the Indians had taken was as clear as the nose on his face; they'd ridden northward. If they had been a band of bloodthirsty Utes, who frequented the territory regularly, they would have ridden south toward one of the Ute villages. Due north lay land frequented by several tribes, not all of them friendly.

Now he had a decision to make, and he didn't like it one bit. He could mount up and follow the trail while it was still fresh, or he could forget the notion and do nothing. But if he didn't go after his friend, Shakespeare might well die and the death would be on his conscience for the rest of his born days.

So he should go.

But, Nate realized, if he rode off in pursuit, there was no way of determining when he would be able to return to his own cabin and his beloved wife. His beloved, *pregnant* wife who was due to deliver their baby in two moons. How could he desert her to go after Shakespeare?

Damn. What a fine pickle this was.

Maybe he should compromise, he decided. He could follow the trail for a short distance and try to ascertain if Shakespeare was with the Indians of his own free will or whether Shakespeare was a captive. The idea appealed to him. He swiftly closed the door to secure the cabin against animal invasion, then swung onto the stallion and took up the chase.

Since the sun was only a few hours above the eastern horizon, he would have plenty of time for tracking the band and still be able to turn back well before dark. He could spend the night in the cabin and head for home in the morning. With his mind made up, he goaded the stallion into a canter, eager to learn more.

The party had continued up the valley, then passed

between two lofty mountains. Another verdant valley stretched before Nate's admiring gaze, and he made a beeline across it as he stuck to the tracks. From the depth of the hoof prints and the long strides the horses had taken, he surmised the Indians were in a hurry to get somewhere. But where?

The band had come on a game trail and promptly changed direction. They were now moving to the northwest, still pushing their mounts.

Nate rode easily, his body flowing in rhythmic motion with the gait of his stallion. He tried not to think of the extra distance he was putting between his wife, Winona, and himself. Surely she would understand if for some reason he came back a day later than anticipated.

Thick woodland hemmed him in on both sides. He idly listened to the cries of animals and the songs of birds, his concentration focused on the trail. Dimly, he recalled Shakespeare advising him time and again to always be aware of the surrounding countryside, to always be alert for movement in all directions. But in his concern and haste he dispelled the memory and simply kept going.

The tracks climbed a gradual slope to a ridge, then went down the other side toward a small, shimmering lake. Nate spotted elk on the shore but they bolted as he drew closer. In the dank earth bordering the lake he found where the Indians had halted to allow their animals to drink. He did the same. Kneeling while the stallion gulped, he touched his fingers to several of the tracks, trying to gauge how far behind the band he was. The manner in which his fingers speared into the earth without making the dirt crumble convinced him he was not more than ten hours or so behind. Good. If he kept pushing, he could probably overtake them within the next day or so.

Nate mounted and resumed the pursuit, traveling

along the west shore of the lake, then entering a thick track of forest that seemed to stretch on forever. It was well past noon when he emerged from the vegetation into a high country meadow. A badger saw him and took flight. So did a doe.

He barely paid any attention to them. Preoccupied with his quest, he soon left the meadow behind and found himself in a region dotted with boulders the size of wagons. The tracks beckoned him ever onward, tantalizing him with the mystery of what lay at the end of the trail. He saw no evidence to indicate Shakespeare had been harmed. Because the mountain man's white mare, like Indian mounts, went unshod, it was difficult to tell which tracks had been made by Shakespeare's horse. Difficult, but not impossible.

The trail skirted another mountain. On the opposite side the direction of travel once more became northwest. Nate racked his brain, trying to remember which tribes dwelt in the land that lay ahead. The Shoshones, of course, the tribe into which he had been adopted by virtue of his marriage to Winona, herself a Shoshone. There were also Bannocks up that way, a tribe as ruthless in its extermination of whites as the widely dreaded Blackfeet. And, if he recollected Shakespeare's teachings correctly, the Nez Perce and the Flathead Indians also staked a claim to some of the land farther to the northwest.

He wound along a sparsely forested valley to a series of hills. The band had gone straight up one and he imitated their example. From the top a wondrous vista unfolded before his appreciative gaze. He could see for many miles no matter which way he turned. His pulse quickened when he spied a group of horsemen far, far to the northwest, crossing a plain. He squinted in the bright sunlight, striving to distinguish details, but the attempt was futile.

Then he heard a faint drumming noise.

For a moment Nate couldn't identify the sound. He cocked his head, listening intently, and belatedly realized the drumming was caused by horses moving at a full gallop—*to his rear.* Twisting, he gasped in surprise at discovering three Indians several hundred yards away, riding hard to overtake him. He recognized their style of dress instantly and goaded the stallion down the hill at a reckless pace, aware that his life hung in the balance if he failed to elude his pursuers.

They were Utes eager for his scalp.

Chapter Two

The big stallion's muscles rippled as it raced to the bottom of the hill and galloped between two others. Nate glanced over his right shoulder at the crest he had just vacated and saw the three Utes appear. One of them vented a savage whoop and the trio surged over the rim.

Facing front, Nate surveyed the terrain, trying to think of a way to shake the warriors. All three carried bows, and he knew from bitter experience that most Indian men were exceptionally adept archers. Warriors were trained from childhood in the use of the bow, and by the time they reached adulthood many could hit a target the size of an apple at fifty yards with consummate ease.

He held his body close to the stallion, trying to make as small a target of himself as possible. The feel of the Hawken in his left hand reassured him a bit. If he could get far enough ahead, he might be able to discourage the three warriors by slaying one.

Beyond the hills lay a grassy meadow. He made a beeline for the forest on the other side, and he was halfway across when he glimpsed the network of earthen burrows in his path. With a start he realized they were prairie dog holes, dozens and dozens of them, and he vividly recalled all the terrible stories he'd heard about careless riders who ventured into prairie dog towns and wound up being unhorsed when their mounts broke a leg and went down.

Nate's mouth went dry at the prospect. He was already among the low mounds. To try to stop would court disaster since slowing the stallion would more likely cause him to step full into a hole. He saw scores of the white-tailed rodents diving for cover, vanishing into their burrows with a flick of their tails while uttering shrill barks.

He did his best to avoid the larger mounds where the holes were obvious, but some holes were in flat ground where they were partially concealed by grass. A prairie dog abruptly darted in front of the stallion and the horse veered sharply to the left. A large mound lay right in their path.

Nate hauled on the reins in a frantic bid to avert catastrophe, but his efforts were in vain. The stallion started to go over the mound when one of its front legs caught in a burrow and it toppled forward. Nate threw himself from the saddle, leaping to the right, clutching the Hawken for dear life. He landed hard on his right shoulder and rolled to his knees, fearing the worst.

The stallion had also hit and rolled, and now the horse lay on its side, dazed, waving its legs and wheezing.

Shoving upright, Nate ran to his animal, fearing one of its legs had sustained a break. He moved around to its head and gripped the bridle, intending to help the horse rise. Then he heard a hateful screech and spun.

Charging toward him were the three Utes, who had fanned out to give themselves room to maneuver and to make it more difficult for him to slay them. They were slightly over one hundred yards off and each warrior already had a shaft nocked to his bowstring.

Nate knew there was no time to try and get the stallion up and ride off. If he attempted the feat, he'd be a pincushion before he traveled a dozen feet. His sole recourse was to fight and hope for the best.

He whipped the Hawken to his right shoulder, cocked the hammer, and took a bead on the centermost Ute. The warrior saw him aim and began swerving from side to side. Stubbornly, he tracked the rider, and when he felt certain he couldn't miss, he fired. At the booming retort lead streaked from the barrel accompanied by a cloud of acrid smoke.

Ninety yards out the middle warrior flung his arms into the air and pitched from his mount.

Nate quickly placed the rifle stock on the ground and went to work reloading, his fingers flying. He didn't want to rely on the pistols just yet. Move! his mind screamed. They're getting closer! He swiftly poured the proper quantity of black powder from his horn into the muzzle, using a crease in his palm as the mark to determine how much powder was sufficient. Then his fingers flew to the ammo pouch and removed a ball and patch. It took all of his self-control to prevent panic from overcoming him. He wrapped the ball in the patch and shoved both into the barrel using his thumb. With a wrenching motion he extracted the ramrod, glancing at his foes as he did.

The Ute on the right let an arrow fly.

Nate saw it coming, saw the glittering tip and the spinning feathers, saw that it had been aimed unerringly. All this he noticed in the span of a second, and even as the shaft arced down toward his chest he nimbly stepped to the right. The arrow thudded into the earth several feet past the spot where he had stood.

He glimpsed the other warrior about to fire and shoved the ramrod down the barrel. Don't stop! he urged himself. Stay calm and keep going. The ramrod tamped the ball home and he yanked the long rod out, let it fall, and pressed the stock to his shoulder once more.

Out of the blue flashed a whizzing arrow.

Acute pain flared in Nate's left shoulder. He looked down to find he'd been hit, creased by the shaft, his shirt and skin torn open. Ignoring the wound, he sighted on the warrior on the right, pulled back the hammer, and squeezed the trigger when the man was sixty yards distant.

The second Ute jerked when struck, then soundlessly toppled.

Only one left, Nate told himself, placing the rifle at his feet. He drew the twin flintlocks, pivoting to confront the last attacker. The Ute had a shaft ready to fly, and as Nate laid eyes on him he did just that.

Darting to the left, Nate extended both pistols. The shaft sped harmlessly past him. He couldn't fire yet, though. Pistols had a limited range and the final Ute was fifty yards away. He had to get closer, and instead of waiting for the warrior to come to him, he charged.

The Ute appeared surprised by the tactic. He was nocking yet another arrow, riding straight for the young mountaineer. In a smooth motion he brought the bow level.

Nate still couldn't fire. Both of his pistols were smoothbore single-shot .55 caliber flintlocks, powerful man-stoppers under thirty yards and forty yards still separated him from his enemy. He ran faster, hoping to shoot before the Ute let the arrow go. But the very next instant, the warrior fired.

Taking one more stride, Nate dived, landing on his elbows and knees, pain jarring his limbs. He was barely aware the shaft had passed harmlessly over his head. All that mattered was ending the battle then and there. From his prone position he held the pistols steady, angled the barrels upward, and when the onrushing Ute materialized in front of both sights, about to loose another arrow, he squeezed both triggers.

The twin balls struck the warrior high in the chest, smacking into his body and lifting him from his horse. He grimaced as he fell, landing flat on his back and not moving again.

Nate lay equally still, catching his breath, trying to calm his nerves. He looked at each Ute; none displayed any hint of life. Then he remembered a crucial lesson he'd learned the hard way, namely to never leave his weapons unloaded for any longer than necessary. A mountaineer could never tell when a new danger might crop up, sometimes immediately on the heels of another.

He rose to his knees and proceeded to reload both flintlocks. Once done, he hurried to retrieve the Hawken and loaded it. As he slid the ramrod back into its housing he looked around for the stallion. To his delight, the horse was not more than fifteen yards to the south, standing still. He ran to the grazing animal and bent down to examine its legs. To his immense relief, none were broken.

Nate straightened and saw the Ute mounts running off to the southwest. He let them go. They were of no use to him and he had more urgent business to attend to. Mounting, he glanced at the corpses. A year ago he would have given them a proper burial. But he'd learned a great deal since coming West, and one of the lessons had been that carrion eaters existed for a reason. Who was he to deprive the coyotes and the buzzards of their food? The good Lord had put such critters on the Earth for a reason, and he wasn't about to buck divine foresight.

Shrugging, still ignoring his flesh-wound, Nate rode hard to the northwest. He eyed the nearby mountains excitedly, seeking the ideal spot. A deer trail leading up the slope of a high peak to his left attracted his attention. He estimated he could climb hundreds of feet before he would need to turn the stallion around, and from such a height he might be able to see the distant party on the far plain.

Up the slope he went, the stallion responding to his guidance. There were trees and high weeds on both sides until he rose above the vegetation and reined up. The plain was visible, but the party was nowhere in sight. Frustrated, he squinted, and at the extreme limit of his vision he spied them, a cluster of riders still bearing to the northwest. For a moment he thought he saw a white horse among the group, and then they were too indistinct for him to note any details at all.

Had he really seen Shakespeare's mare, or had his eyes played tricks on him? Nate frowned, debating what to do next. If he pressed the stallion to its limit, he might overtake that party by tomorrow afternoon at the very latest. It meant another day's delay in returning to Winona, but if Shakespeare was indeed in trouble, then he owed it to his best friend to make a rescue attempt.

The decision sparked prompt action. He turned the stallion and went to the bottom of the mountain, then headed toward the plain. Now that he had a definite destination in mind, he stuck to as straight a route as possible given the ruggedness of the terrain.

Slowly the day waned, the golden sun climbing ever

higher in the blue sky and dipping toward the western horizon. The shadows lengthened. As evening approached, deer and elk came out to feed in larger numbers.

Nate ignored them. He was too concerned over Shakespeare to think about food. Reaching that plain before nightfall became his singular goal. His thoughts strayed as he rode, dwelling on the beautiful woman he proudly called his wife and his anxiety over the impending birth. He'd never been a father, but he knew that childbirth could be dangerous for a woman, knew that many women died in delivery. The idea of such a fate befalling Winona was too horrible to contemplate, but contemplate it he had, which was one of the reasons he'd gone to visit Shakespeare.

The mountain man had been married before and must know all about the act of giving birth, Nate reasoned. He figured he could ask his mentor for advice on how best to guarantee Winona's delivery went without a hitch. There must be something he could do. When he'd broached the subject with Winona, she had bestowed one of her enigmatic wifely smiles on him and advised him not to worry, that she knew what to do and everything would be fine. So he'd bluntly asked her how she intended to deliver the baby by herself, and her answer had shocked him to his core.

"Indian women have been giving birth since the dawn of time," Winona had explained in the manner she might adopt to instruct a six-year old child. "I will go outside when the baby is ready, find a quiet spot in the woods, squat, and the baby will be born."

Nate had mistakenly believed she was joking and laughed. Her eyes had flashed in the manner they often did when he made a fool of himself, and he'd realized she was serious. "Dear God. You don't mean it?" he'd blurted.

"Is something wrong?" Winona had responded rather indignantly.

"Are you telling me that Shoshone women always go off by themselves to have babies? They must have help of some kind."

"Well, yes, we do."

"I knew it."

"We usually squat next to a sapling so we can grip the tree as tight as we want. It helps us when we push the baby from our womb."

"A tree?" Nate had repeated in amazement.

"Yes. How do white women give birth?"

"They lie in bed, as any sensible person would, and they have a doctor come to help them. If a doctor isn't available, then they get a midwife or a friend or two to help out."

Winona had stared at him in evident confusion. "White women give birth on their *backs?*"

"Certainly. Why?"

"But a baby must come out from between a woman's legs. It is so much easier if the woman is upright. Then the baby's own weight helps to bring it into this world. Why, the way you describe it, the woman must push and push to get the baby out," Winona had said, and then blinked as if in sudden comprehension. "Perhaps that is the reason white women need so much help."

"I'd be a lot more comfortable if *we* had some help," Nate had said.

Winona had laughed. "Since when does a Shoshone woman need help in using her body in the manner in which the Great Mystery intended it?"

Nate's cheeks flushed with embarrassment at the memory of that conversation. He hadn't been able to come up with a good answer for her, and now she was intent on delivering the baby alone. Why did women have to be so obstinate all the time? If there was one other lesson he'd learned since setting off on his own, it was an observation most men seemed to share: Women were damned peculiar.

He chuckled at the notion and absently scanned the forest ahead. By his reckoning he should reach the plain within an hour. He went around a thicket, over a knoll, and along a stream. Birds were chirping nearby and a squirrel chattered at him from a high tree. The tranquility lulled him into complacency, so he didn't notice the creature eyeing him hungrily until a bestial snarl rent the air and he glanced to his left to behold the terror of the Rocky Mountains, the scourge of every Indian and white man alike.

Lumbering toward him was a mighty grizzly bear.

Chapter Three

Nate urged the stallion into a race for its life, watching the bear charge and dreading the consequences should the horse falter. He'd tangled with grizzlies before and knew from firsthand experience why they were so formidable. Adult males weighed 1400 pounds or more and possessed five long claws on each paw that could be used to slash flesh to ribbons with a single swipe. And although grizzlies walked with a slow, clumsy gait, when necessary they could run as fast as a horse.

Now Nate found that out the hard way. He saw the grizzly gaining and goaded the stallion to greater speed. Since trying to shoot the grizzly while galloping on horseback would be a waste of the ball, unless by some miracle he hit an eye or the heart, he didn't bother to fire. He knew its thick skull protected the bear's brain from all but shots fired at very close range.

He could see the bear's sides heaving as the brute

ran. A pronounced hump above its shoulders distinguished the terrible beast from its lesser cousin, the black bear. The concave face, enormous in its own right, was set in feral determination.

Not this time! Nate thought, hunching over in the saddle.

On three prior occasions he'd been forced to fight grizzlies; once, while en route from St. Louis to the Rockies with his Uncle Zeke; again, when on the way to the 1828 rendezvous just last summer; and the third time while off with Shakespeare learning how to trap beaver. All three times he'd barely survived the encounters.

Thinking of those attacks brought to mind the Indian name bestowed on him by a Cheyenne warrior who witnessed the first scrape. 'Grizzly Killer,' the Indians now called him in honor of his prowess. Although, if it had been up to him, he would gladly have avoided each run-in with the fierce beasts. Having an Indian name was fine, but gaining it had nearly cost his life.

The grizzly vented a furious roar.

Nate looked back, elated to find the stallion had pulled out well ahead of the bear. Grizzlies weren't able to sustain their top speed for any great distance, so the stallion's stamina would prove the determining factor. He stared anxiously down at the ground, afraid there might be more prairie dog burrows in his path, but the ground was level and clear.

After a minute the grizzly gave up the chase and slowed to a disgruntled walk. It glared at the departing horse as if indignant that any animal would decline the privilege of being its main course.

Laughing in delight, Nate straightened and continued toward the plain. But he was more alert, constantly scanning the countryside for bears. Grizzlies were everywhere in the Rockies and the Plains, and their aggressive temperaments made them the most dangerous creatures in the wilderness.

The sun sank below the horizon and twilight enveloped the landscape. Still Nate pressed ahead, and the shadows had merged into an inky blanket by the time he ultimately reached his destination.

At the southern edge of the plain he halted, planning to make camp right there, but the stallion raised its head and sniffed loudly, then tapped one hoof on the ground, seemingly eager to keep going. He gave it a free rein and the horse cut to the right, traveled fifteen yards, and stopped beside a small spring.

Nate patted the stallion's neck in gratitude. "Always trust your horse's instincts," Shakespeare had once advised him, and the admonition had proven remarkably beneficial. He climbed down and let the stallion drink.

Should he make a fire or not? Nate mused, and decided against the notion. Campfires stood out like sore thumbs in the vast sea of benighted forest, and for all he knew the party he'd seen might spot his. He had plenty of jerked venison in his saddlebags and fresh water to drink. A fire wasn't necessary, although he was tempted to start one just so he could spend a few hours reading his copy of James Fenimore Cooper's latest book. He'd already read *THE LAST OF THE MOHICANS* once and liked it so much he'd begun reading it again.

He stripped off the saddlebags and the saddle, then tied the stallion to a nearby tree using a twenty-foot length of rope so the horse could graze at its leisure. Not tying a horse in Indian country was downright foolish, since the animal might wander off or Indians might steal it. The trappers had a saying along those lines: "It's better to count ribs than to count tracks."

Which meant it was wiser to let a horse go a little hungry by limiting its grazing space rather than let it loose to roam and not have it in the morning.

He took a handful of venison from the saddlebags, spread his blanket near the water, and settled down for the night. From near and far arose the sounds of animals; the deep coughs of panthers, the hoots of owls, the howling of wolves, and the yipping of coyotes. Stars filled the heavens, more than he had ever seen at any one time in New York City, and he propped his head on his left hand to admire the celestial spectacle.

Nate wondered about Winona, hoping she was well. He felt slightly guilty over leaving her to visit Shakespeare, but the trip had to be made. Besides her upcoming delivery, there was the matter of the guns to discuss.

Recently three men had tried to trade crates of rifles to the Utes in exchange for prime beaver pelts. Had they been successful, the Utes would have acquired the firepower necessary to become the dominant tribe in the Rockies. Only through sheer chance had Nate discovered their greedy scheme and thwarted it. Now all three were dead and he had the crates safely buried near his cabin. He hoped Shakespeare could give him advice on what to do with the guns.

He finished the jerked meat and drank heartily from the spring. He could hear the stallion munching on grass, and deep in the forest an animal shrieked in pain, perhaps under attack by a predator. Laying down again, he pondered his predicament and debated whether to turn around by tomorrow night if he failed to overtake the riders he'd spotted. Gradually his eyelids drooped and he entered the realm of dreams, although in his case they were nightmares. Once he imagined Shakespeare being hacked to bits by a band of hostiles wielding butcher knives, and later he dreamed that Winona had fallen and hurt herself and was calling his name over and over in vain.

The chirping and raucous cries of countless birds roused him from slumber before the sun rose. He sat up, listening to them greet the dawn in their own cheery manner, then rose and stretched. The stallion eyed him expectantly. He led it to the spring, chewed on a piece of venison while it drank, then saddled up. Twenty minutes after opening his eyes he was on the way again.

Nate found the tracks left by the band and followed them. Crossing the plain took hours; the sun was high by the time he reached a tract of woodland and found where the band had paralleled a stream for a spell. In a spacious clearing he came on the warm embers of a dying fire, the site where the band had camped for the night. The find encouraged him. It meant he was closer to them than expected.

He pressed onward, noting the riders were continuing to bear generally to the northwest. Unfortunately, the mystery party left no clues behind as to their identity beyond the obvious fact they were Indians.

At noon he was deep in mountains again. He halted for a brief break, eating more jerky and allowing the stallion to rest. Then he mounted and headed out.

After he covered two more miles, a high ridge appeared. The trail wound along its base, bearing westward because the riders skirted it, but he altered direction and rode to the top of the ridge in the hope of seeing them. No sooner did he rein up than his persistence was rewarded.

Eleven men were less than a quarter of a mile away, camped at the edge of a meadow. He spied a white horse that might or might not be Shakespeare's. Grinning, he retraced his path to the bottom. The Indians, not expecting pursuit, had stopped for an extended midday rest. Now he would find out what was going on.

He rode to the west end of the ridge, then warily moved into dense woodland beyond. The meadow wasn't more than a couple of hundred yards off and he exercised the utmost caution as he drew within half that distance and dismounted. After tying the stallion to a low limb, he hefted the Hawken and stealthily advanced until he could see figures moving through the trees.

Nate crouched, going from trunk to trunk, studiously avoiding all twigs and branches in his path. Twenty yards from the band he eased onto his stomach and proceeded to crawl. He glimpsed Indians whose style of dress seemed oddly familiar, although try as he might he couldn't place them. Then he spotted Shakespeare.

He halted in surprise, his eyes narrowing. The mountain man was conversing with two warriors. Shakespeare's hands weren't tied, but Nate noticed something odd. His friend wasn't carrying any weapons, not even a knife. Since no mountaineer in his right mind would go anywhere unarmed, Nate concluded the Indians had taken his mentor's firearms and butcher knife. But if so, and acting on the logical assumption Shakespeare was their prisoner, why had the warriors not bound him? At the very least Nate expected to find his friend's wrists bound.

It made no sense.

Perplexed, Nate inched nearer until he was within ten feet of the band, lying partially concealed under the low limbs of a small pine tree. Another fact struck him as strange. Previously, the warriors had been heading northwest at a rapid clip. Yet now they were idly conversing as if they didn't have a care in the world and weren't in any great hurry to reach their destination.

Nate scanned the entire group, striving to piece together some rhyme or reason to their behavior. His brain abruptly shrieked a warning and he felt that something was very, very wrong, but he couldn't isolate the cause. He studied the Indians, even more closely.

And then he saw it.

With a start Nate realized there were only eight warriors present now, not ten. Where were the other two? He looked right and left and saw no indication of them. Between the time he'd spotted the whole band from the ridge and his arrival at the meadow, the pair had disappeared. He figured they must be in the woods hunting for game.

Thank goodness he hadn't blundered into them!

He saw Shakespeare peer into the forest and frown. Why? The idea of signaling his friend occurred to him but he discarded the notion as too dangerous. One of the Indians might see him. He crossed his forearms and rested his chin on them, the Hawken at his right side.

A tall Indian approached McNair. He wore fine buckskins and had long, dark, braided hair flecked with spots of gray and adorned with four eagle feathers. Instead of a bow, which was far more common among warriors of all tribes, he cradled a flintlock rifle in his arms.

Nate figured the warrior must be a prominent member of the tribe. The man stopped and addressed Shakespeare, and to Nate's utter amazement the warrior spoke English.

"It will not be long now, Carcajou."

The name was familiar to Nate. It was the French word for the wolverine, a denizen of the Rockies reputed to be every bit as fierce as the grizzly, and the name by which several of the tribes referred to the white-haired mountain man. He saw Shakespeare glare at the speaker, then respond bitterly.

"May all your male children become women."

One of the other warriors laughed.

The tall Indian took the insult in stride. He sighed and gazed into the distance. "How long will you be mad at me, my brother?"

"For as long as the sun shines," Shakespeare replied. "And don't call me your brother, Buffalo Horn. You are the lowest, meanest son of a bitch who ever lived and I hope the Blackfeet take your hair real soon."

Nate was astounded his friend would use such language. Indian men adhered to a strong unwritten code of honor and dignity, and they rarely tolerated personal insults. Then, to compound his confusion, the tall warrior and the same one who had laughed before both did so.

This other warrior, a lean man with a hooked nose and a pointed chin, wagged the war club he held and said, "You know a man must be true to his word. Whether white or Indian, a man's word is a measure of his worth as a human being."

Shakespeare bristled. "If I wasn't so outnumbered I'd teach you about worth, Running Elk, you polecat."

Buffalo Horn made a gesture as if to say that talking with McNair was a waste of time. "We have been through that once."

"Don't remind me," Shakespeare said.

"I never thought I would live to see the day when *you* would turn your back on your word," Buffalo Horn declared. "And after all that happened."

"It happened twenty years ago, damn your hide," Shakespeare snapped. "You can't expect to hold me to it after so much time has passed."

"It is out of my hands," Buffalo Horn said solemnly.

"I'll remember you for this," Shakespeare promised. "Some day, some way, I'll get even."

Nate wished one of them would drop a clue as to the topic of their discussion. He had no idea what was going on. Sliding forward several inches, he cocked his head to listen better. So well that he distinctly heard the click of a hammer being cocked. A heartbeat later he felt the barrel of a gun jab into the nape of his neck.

Chapter Four

Nate froze, knowing the slightest move would prove fatal. He heard someone snicker, and then a pair of moccasin covered feet stepped into view. The gun barrel, however, never moved, which indicated there were two of them. The two missing warriors, he figured.

A young warrior squatted in front of him. Smiling, he wagged a tomahawk he held in his right hand, then motioned for Nate to rise.

Bewildered, Nate complied. The pressure on his neck disappeared, and a second warrior moved around in front of him. This one held a cocked fusee, one of the inferior trade rifles the Indians received from the fur companies in exchange for prime pelts. While fusees lacked the range of conventional long guns, they were every bit as lethal pinned in one's neck.

The warrior with the tomahawk leaned forward and picked up the Hawken. Rising, he removed both of

Nate's pistols, the butcher knife, and Nate's tomahawk. He admired the weapons for a bit, then jerked
his thumb toward the camp.

Incensed at himself for being taken so easily, Nate
walked forward. The other Indians heard him coming,
as did Shakespeare, and they turned to regard him
with a mixture of curiosity and amusement, but no
hostility.

The mountain man placed his hands on his hips and
declared testily, "I thought I taught you better than
this. How could you let yourself be taken by these
half-wits?"

"I was about to ask the same thing of you," Nate
retorted, annoyed at the brusque greeting. After all
the trouble he had gone to, he felt a friendly smile at
the very least was in order.

A hearty laugh burst from Buffalo Horn. "The cub
has a point, Carcajou. What is your answer?"

Shakespeare snorted indignantly. "I have a valid
excuse. You curs sneaked into my cabin while I was
reading and got the drop on me. Otherwise, I wouldn't
be here."

Running Elk grinned. "And we should thank you
for leaving your door open. Otherwise, we could never
have sneaked in."

"Grind a man's face in it, why don't you?" Shakespeare snapped, and glancing at Nate he encompassed
all of the band in a single sweep of his arm. "Go, bind
thou up yon dangling apricots, which, like unruly
children, make their sire stoop with oppression of
their prodigal weight: Give some supportance to the
bending twigs. Go thou, and like an executioner, cut
off the heads of too fast growing sprays, that look too
lofty in our commonwealth."

Nate knew his mentor had quoted William Shakespeare again, although he had no idea from which play

the quote stemmed. He saw Buffalo Horn and Running Elk exchange grins and shook his head in confusion.

The warrior who had confiscated Nate's weapons stepped forward and placed them at Buffalo Horn's feet. A short discussion in their native tongue ensued, after which the two warriors responsible for his capture hastened back into the forest.

"They will find your horse and bring it here," Buffalo Horn addressed Nate. "You will need it on the long ride ahead."

"What long ride?" Nate asked, and faced his mentor. "Do you mind telling me what in blazes is going on?"

"What's to explain?" Shakespeare rejoined. "It should be obvious. We're in the clutches of savages who will likely take our hair."

Buffalo Horn hissed like an angry viper. "That is not true and you well know it, McNair. We will not harm a hair on either of you." He paused and smirked. "Unless you try to escape, of course."

"Heathen devil," Shakespeare muttered, and walked a few yards to the west, turning his back on the Indians.

Stepping to his friend's side, Nate placed a hand on Shakespeare's shoulder. "None of this makes any sense to me. You seem to know these Indians. Who are they?"

"Flatheads," Shakespeare snapped distastefully.

Suddenly Nate recollected where he had seen such Indians before; at the last rendezvous. Various tribes attended the rowdy annual event to trade, sell women, or participate in the contests of marksmanship, horse riding, and other skills. "The same ones who were at the rendezvous?" he inquired, studying them.

"No, a different bunch," Shakespeare said. "Buffalo

Horn and these others are from another village. They weren't at the rendezvous because they're afraid to travel so near to Blackfoot country."

Nate glanced at Buffalo Horn, who had overheard the remark, and saw the Indian scowl.

"Again you lie, McNair," the warrior declared. "We have been at the rendezvous every year except last year, when we could not come because of a council we were holding with the Nez Perce. Why must you keep trying to make me mad?"

"Because I'm hoping you'll take a swing at me so I can break your jaw," Shakespeare responded.

Buffalo Horn looked at Nate. "Please forgive his manners, Mr. King. Most men would not treat their brother-in-law with such disrespect."

"Brother-in-law?" Nate said in astonishment, then realized the Flathead had called him by name. "Wait a minute. How is it that you know me?"

"Shakespeare has told us much about you," Buffalo Horn said. "He told us you are not like most whites. You respect our way of life and the earth on which all men must live. He says you are a mighty warrior and generations to come will remember you."

"He did?" Nate blurted in surprise.

"I was exaggerating," Shakespeare said defensively. "I was trying to convince them to let me go. Told them you'd be after them if they didn't." He snorted again. "I had no idea you'd practically walk into their hands."

"They found me by accident," Nate said.

"Accident, hell. Running Elk saw you on that ridge back yonder," Shakespeare stated. "They deliberately dawdled here to give you a chance to make a fool of yourself. And you accommodated them."

"They set a trap for me?"

The mountain man nodded. "Buffalo Horn sent

two men into the trees to wait for you to show up. He told them to take you alive, otherwise you'd be bald right about now."

Nate felt like a prize dunderhead. He glanced at the forest to discover his two captors returning with his black stallion, then at Buffalo Horn, the man who claimed to be McNair's brother-in-law. The thought jogged his memory. "Didn't you once tell me that you were married to a Flathead woman a long time ago?"

"I may have."

"Was the woman Buffalo Horn's sister?"

"Unfortunately."

Nate's confusion doubled. When a white man married an Indian woman, the tribe usually adopted the groom as one of their own, just as the Shoshones had done with him. If the Flatheads had done likewise with Shakespeare, why were they taking him against his will? And to where? He posed the question to Buffalo Horn.

"We are on our way to our village," the warrior answered. "You are welcome to come, if you like. If not, and if you give your word that you will not interfere with what must be done, we will give you back your weapons and allow you to ride off."

"Just like that?"

"My people have never taken the life of a white man and there is no reason for us to take yours," Buffalo Horn said. "We have always been friendly to all whites. When trappers come to our village, we feed them and let them stay in our lodges. Even though many of them treat us as inferiors, we know that all men are brothers."

Nate didn't know what to say.

"My people are as friendly to whites as your wife's people, the Shoshones," Buffalo Horn went on.

"You know about my wife, then?"

"Carcajou told us."

Shifting, Nate regarded his mentor critically. "Is there anything you *didn't* tell them?"

Shakespeare made a show of placing a palm to his forehead and feigning hurt feelings. "Thy wit is a very bitter sweeting. It is a most sharp sauce."

Buffalo Horn took a step toward Nate. "Do you understand him when he talks like that?"

"Sometimes," Nate said.

"I never do," the Flathead said. "I think he does it just to upset other people."

"Probably," Nate agreed, and added, "You speak excellent English, though. Where did you learn it so well?"

"Carcajou taught me during the years he lived in our village."

"And me," Running Elk chimed in.

The grizzled mountain man sighed. "That's what I get for being so blamed considerate. I taught them the language, and now they use it to mock me and treat me like buffalo *crap.*"

"We do no such thing," Buffalo Horn said, and looked at Nate. "Now, what about you, Grizzly Killer? Do we have your promise you will not try to stop us from taking McNair to our village?"

"Are you fixing to harm him?"

"No."

Shakespeare pivoted and jabbed a finger at the warrior. "Now who is lying? You have the most horrible fate any man can face lined up for me. Why, I'd rather be skinned alive or eaten by a grizzly."

"You exaggerate again," Buffalo Horn said.

Nate couldn't take the suspense any longer. "What *is* the fate in store for him? Just what the hell is going on, anyway?"

Buffalo Horn went to answer when another brave

called out in the Flathead tongue and pointed to the southeast. Every warrior whirled.

Glancing in the same direction, Nate felt his breath catch in his throat at seeing over two dozen riders on the very same ridge he'd been on when he first spied the Flatheads. He could tell they were Indians and hoped they were friendly, but a single word uttered by Running Elk proved otherwise.

"Utes."

The Flatheads scrambled for their mounts even as the band of Utes vented war whoops and surged down the ridge toward them. Shakespeare ran to his white horse and swiftly mounted.

Nate found himself standing alone, not a yard from his weapons, the only one still on foot. He glanced at his rifle, wondering if the Flatheads would stop him if he made a grab for it.

Buffalo Horn moved his horse closer. "Pick up your guns. If those Utes catch us, they will torture us to death."

In a stride Nate was bending down to hastily reclaim all of his arms. In seconds the pistols, knife, and tomahawk were again around his waist and the Hawken in his left hand. He swung onto the stallion and noted with surprise that every Flathead had waited for him.

Barking words in the Flathead tongue, Buffalo Horn led the band to the northwest at a gallop.

Nate fell in beside Shakespeare, his stallion easily keeping pace. He was glad he'd opted to bring the big black instead of his mare. Recently acquired from the same trappers who had tried to trade rifles to the Utes, the stallion possessed remarkable strength and endurance.

The Flatheads quickly crossed the meadow and entered woodland on the far side, staying clustered together, each warrior riding with an air of grim resolve about him.

Glancing at his mentor, Nate saw the same expression on his friend. He knew from prior experience that Indians were capable of perpetrating atrocities every bit as grisly as any ever practiced by white men, especially where warring tribes were concerned. Buffalo Horn had understated the situation. Any Flathead who fell behind or was captured would die a horrible death.

He wondered why the Utes were at least a day's ride north of their normal range, and an answer occurred to him that made him stiffen in surprise. He might be the reason. If those three Utes he'd slain were part of a larger war party, when the other Utes found the bodies they would have set out to track the culprit down. They had tracked him to the top of the ridge and spied the Flatheads.

Damn. It was all his fault.

Nate concentrated on the task at hand, threading among the trees with the same skill as his Indian companions. He saw Buffalo Horn look back at him two or three times. Why? And what would the Flathead do once they eluded the Utes? Try to take his weapons again? He wasn't going to permit it, no matter what.

As the chase continued, the Flatheads were goaded on by the distant whoops of their fierce mortal enemies. When the forest gave way to a series of hills, Running Elk took the lead in winding among them.

Looking over his shoulder, Nate was startled to find four of the Utes had pulled out well ahead of the rest and were closing the gap rapidly.

Running Elk skirted a hill and, hemmed in on both sides by high rock walls, entered a ravine. The rest promptly followed.

Nate didn't like being boxed in. Should the Utes gain the rim, the Flatheads would be easy to pick off. So, for that matter, would Shakespeare and he. Nate avoided a boulder in his path and saw Running Elk bear to the right as the ravine curved. Seconds later he galloped around the turn and was stunned to discover the Flatheads bunched together at the base of another stone wall.

The ravine was a dead end.

Chapter Five

Nate hauled sharply on the reins to avoid colliding with the Flatheads in front of him. The black stopped almost instantly, jerking its head up within inches of another animal's rump. He heard thundering hooves to his rear and glanced back to see one of the warriors stop almost on top of him. For a few moments confusion reigned. The Flatheads were talking excitedly in their own tongue, some pointing at the high walls.

All Nate could think of was the Ute war party rapidly drawing closer. He brought the stallion around, motioning for the nearest warriors to move their animals so he could accomplish the feat, and glanced at his friend.

Shakespeare had done the same. "We've got to get out of here," he stated somberly.

Nate nodded. He felt the same sense of dire urgency. The Utes would reach the mouth of the ravine soon, if they hadn't already, and he wasn't too fond of the notion of fighting his way through them in the cramped confines of the rocky defile. Thank goodness he had the pistols; they would give him a slight edge. He started to move past the milling Flatheads, glancing over his shoulder at Buffalo Horn. "I'll take the lead," he offered. "Have your people ride hard on my heels."

"Wait for me," Shakespeare said, and looked at the tall warrior. "I want my weapons, damn you, and I want them now."

Buffalo Horn frowned and hesitated.

"I need a chance to defend myself, don't I?" Shakespeare demanded angrily.

Demonstrating marked reluctance, Buffalo Horn snapped instructions at another warrior, who then moved his horse over beside Shakespeare's and handed over the mountain man's rifle, pistol, and knife.

Shakespeare beamed as he reclaimed his weapons. "I should thank the Utes for this," he said in delight.

"Ready?" Nate asked impatiently, eager to be off before the Utes had them trapped.

Nodding, Shakespeare hefted his rifle and gripped his reins tightly. "Advance our standards, set upon our foes. Our ancient word of courage, fair Saint George, inspire us with the spleen of fiery dragons! Upon them! Victory sits on our helms," he roared, and grinned. *"King Richard III."*

Nate shook his head and goaded the stallion into a gallop. Sometimes he wondered if his good friend had been struck on the head as a child. He discarded the train of thought to concentrate on the critical matter at hand. Behind him came Shakespeare and the Flatheads, the pounding of their horses echoing off the stone walls.

Had the Utes reached the ravine? That was the crucial factor. Nate tensed as he came to the turn and raced around it to see his worst fears realized.

The four Utes who had pulled ahead of their fellows were just entering the narrow chasm. They spied the onrushing frontiersman immediately and voiced strident cries. A hundred yards to their rear, coming on strong, was the rest of the war party.

Nate never let the stallion break stride. He leaned forward, a fiery resolve fueling his being, and tucked the Hawken's stock into his right shoulder. Aiming on horseback was difficult under the best of circumstances, and Nate found the task harder while weaving among the boulders scattered in his path. He saw the Utes stop as three of the warriors frantically tried to nock shafts to their bow strings and the fourth wagged a war club overhead. Good. The Flatheads would have momentum working in their favor when they crashed into their foes.

He took a bouncing bead on the foremost Ute, a stocky man armed with a bow, and when only ten feet from the quartet he fired. His ball bored into the Ute's face just as the warrior raised a bow, catapulting the stocky figure off his horse. Nate sped onward, holding the rifle and the reins in one hand while he drew a pistol with the other.

From behind him came the blast of Shakespeare's rifle and a second Ute toppled.

Nate was on the remaining twosome before he could so much as blink. A war club swooped at his head and he ducked under the blow, extending his pistol at the same instant and sending a ball into the Ute's forehead. And then he was past the ravine mouth, temporarily in the clear. Temporarily, because he was now hemmed in by hills on each side and charging toward him was the rest of the war party, in the same gap, not seventy yards away.

Going straight would be certain suicide. Nate cut to

the right, heading up the slope, his body held low over the stallion's back as the animal's powerful legs drove them upward. A backward glance showed Shakespeare and the Flatheads following his example. Lying in the ravine were the bodies of the four Utes. Not one Flathead had been slain . . . yet.

Nate looked at the Utes. They were galloping up the hill on an intercept course, but the steep slope was slowing them down, just as it impeded his stallion. He wedged the spent pistol under his belt and kept going. The top of the hill was fifty feet off, yet seemed to be a mile. Focusing on the rim, he rode like a madman.

The Utes were shrieking loud enough to be heard clear back in Missouri.

In less than half a minute the black stallion attained the crest, and Nate paused to mark the progress of his friends and his foes. Shakespeare and the Flatheads were right behind him, the Utes thirty feet below. He whipped out the second pistol, tilted the barrel to compensate for the distance and the elevation, and fired, not really expecting to score a hit but to deter the war party.

One of the foremost riders threw out his arms and fell with a scream.

Five down, Nate mentally noted, but the Utes still outnumbered his allies. Jamming the flintlock underneath his belt, he spun the stallion and headed for the far side. Shakespeare and several of the Flatheads were ahead of him, and the mountain man sped over the rim a heartbeat later. He found himself riding beside Running Elk, and the two of them rode even with one another as they left the top and galloped down the opposite slope. Even steeper on this side, Nate had to dig his feet into his stirrups to keep from being unhorsed.

At the bottom lay a plain, and Nate breathed a sigh

of relief as the stallion hit the level ground and went all out, passing several of the Flatheads. In short order he was again next to his mentor.

Shakespeare grinned at him, as if enjoying every second of their harrowing ordeal. "This is the life!" he shouted.

Nate didn't bother responding. As far as he was concerned, he much preferred a quiet evening home alone with Winona to racing pell-mell through the wilderness with bloodthirsty Utes on his tail.

For minutes the chase continued, the Utes not more than thirty yards behind. The plain ended, replaced by verdant forest, which in turn gave way to an arid tract of dusty red earth marred by deep ruts.

Twisting in his saddle, Nate was overjoyed to find the Utes had fallen even farther behind. He faced front as Shakespeare changed direction slightly, making to the northwest where high peaks dominated the landscape, and emulated him. The prospect of finding themselves in another ravine or box canyon caused his stomach muscles to tighten, and he prayed that Shakespeare knew what he was doing.

They attained the mountains without mishap. By now all the animals were tiring and the pace had flagged considerably. Skirting the base of the first peak in the range, Shakespeare swung into a wide gully.

Nate got the impression his friend was heading for a specific destination. Even so, he gazed nervously at the stone walls. To his relief, when only halfway into the gully the mountain man suddenly reined to the right toward a narrow opening. He was forced to ride directly behind Shakespeare as they entered since there wasn't room for both of them. A rocky trail led from the gully floor to the top of the north wall, and once up there he looked toward the entrance where the Utes had yet to appear.

Shakespeare swung off his mount and motioned for Nate to do the same. "Don't just sit there! Reload!"

Insight dawned, and Nate promptly dismounted and hastily commenced reloading all three of his weapons.

The Flatheads joined them, swinging down and moving to the lip of the wall where they crouched and nocked arrows in preparation for the ambush.

As Buffalo Horn went to walk past Shakespeare, the mountain man grabbed the warrior's arm. "Where the blazes are my powder horn and ammo pouch? I need to reload my rifle."

The tall Flathead pointed at another warrior, who had Shakespeare's items slanted across his slim chest, and motioned for them to be returned to their rightful owner.

All this Nate absently took in as he reloaded, his fingers flying. He finished with the Hawken and reached for a flintlock when the drumming hooves of their enemies heralded the arrival of the Utes in the gully. With no time to lose, he dashed to the lip and knelt, staying low to avoid detection.

The Utes were pushing their mounts to the limit. Having lost ground during the last few miles, they were apparently trying to make it up. They galloped down the gully without once gazing up at the top of the walls.

Nate tingled in nervous expectation. He cocked the hammer, his gaze glued to the war party, watching the lead riders. Dust kicked into the air by the Flatheads' mounts still hung in small clouds, rendering it difficult for the Utes to see tracks. A few were trying to do just that, bending down as they rode.

The Flatheads had their bows ready, except for two men who held fusees and Buffalo Horn with his rifle.

When the Utes were almost to the side opening, a warrior in the lead glanced in that direction, saw it, and shouted. The Utes were now twenty feet away and fifteen feet below the rim.

Rising, Buffalo Horn took aim and fired. It was the signal for the other Flatheads to do the same. A shower of arrows and lead poured down onto the hapless Utes, piercing torsos, spearing through necks, or striking limbs.

Nate sighted on the Ute who appeared to be in charge of the war party, the one who had spotted the opening. He took his time, wanting to be sure, holding his breath so he could keep the rifle steady, and fired as the Ute went to turn. The man clutched at his face, then pitched to the ground.

Eight of the Utes were lying in the dirt now. Shakespeare's Hawken cracked and a ninth fell. The survivors were desperately striving to flee, bumping into one another, their mounts spooked by the gunfire, the bodies underfoot, and the dust rising to choke the gully.

Shakespeare cackled in delight.

More and more arrows streaked into the disorganized Utes, their razor barbs slicing through flesh as readily as a Bowie through butter. Three more warriors were sprawled in the dirt before the rest finally got underway, racing for the entrance to the gully in stark fear for their lives, jostling each other in their anxious haste to be the first to escape the slaughter.

Nate didn't fire again. He'd wanted to stop the Utes as much as anyone there, but the one-sided massacre disgusted him. Shakespeare's rifle cracked almost in his very ear and yet another Ute hit the dirt. He shifted to see the Flatheads dashing to their mounts so they could give chase. Let them, he reflected. He had no craving for more killing. Instead, he reloaded the Hawken and both pistols, observing the next stage in the drama from where he knelt.

He saw the Flatheads burst from the side opening

and ride to the fallen Utes. To his surprise, the Flatheads stopped and jumped down. They weren't going to chase the rest of the war party, after all. Aghast, he observed them draw their knives and tomahawks and set to work on the dead and injured with a vengeance. Every body was repeatedly stabbed or hacked. Fingers were chopped from hands; noses and ears from heads; abdomens were ripped open and the entrails strewn about; and scalps were taken with the most savage joy imaginable. The Flatheads became spattered with blood and gore from their own grisly handiwork. Nate felt his stomach flutter and feared he might be sick.

"Not a pretty sight, is it?"

Nate started and turned to find his mentor regarding him carefully. "Revolting is more like it," he said, and stood, adjusting the flintlocks on either side of his belt buckle, the Hawken in his left hand.

"I figured you would be accustomed to this by now," Shakespeare said.

"I doubt I ever will."

"Then there's hope for you yet," the mountain man said with a snicker.

Nate wasn't sure if he'd been insulted or not. "And what about you?" he retorted. "You seemed to think this was all great fun. Weren't you in the least bit afraid for your life?"

Shakespeare launched into another quote from his favorite author. "My lord, wise men ne'er sit and wail their woes, but presently prevent the ways to wail. To fear the foe, since fear oppresseth strength, gives in your weakness strength unto your foe, and so your follies fight against yourself. Fear, and be slain; no worse can come to fight. And fight and die is death destroying death; where fearing dying pays death servile breadth."

"I don't have the foggiest notion what you're babbling about," Nate said testily.

Sighing, Shakespeare stared at the butchery transpiring in the gully. "When you've lived as many years as I have, Nate, you'll learn to take each moment as it comes and to fully appreciate whatever that moment brings."

"Oh? I seem to recall you're not very appreciative of the fact the Flatheads want to take you to their village."

"That's different."

"How so?"

Shakespeare looked Nate in the eyes. "They're taking me there to get married."

Chapter Six

"Get married!" Nate blurted in amazement.

A shadow seemed to descend over Shakespeare's weathered features. He nodded and said softly, "Oh, I am fortune's fool."

Bewildered, Nate idly gazed into the gully and saw Buffalo Horn decapitating one of the Utes. He watched the Flathead chop at the vanquished warrior's neck for a moment, then looked at his mentor. "You have some explaining to do."

Shakespeare stared off into the distance, his lips compressed, his brow knit in contemplation.

"When I found your cabin in a shambles, I figured you were in mortal danger," Nate went on. "I came all this way just to rescue you. You have no idea what I went through, and now you tell me that you're only going off to get married?"

"Unless I mount up and run," Shakespeare said, shifting to survey the mutilation taking place below them.

Nate realized that his friend was serious, and it shocked him. He'd never imagined Shakespeare would run from anything. There must be more to the situation. He realized both of them could slip away if they wanted since the Flatheads were totally preoccupied. "I'll go if you do," he said.

Shakespeare gazed at their horses, then back into the gully. He hefted his rifle, took a stride toward his mount, and abruptly halted. "Damn!" he snapped, and angrily slapped his thigh.

"What is the matter with you?" Nate asked, completely mystified. He'd never seen the mountain man behave in such a peculiar fashion, never known McNair to be the least bit indecisive.

"I can't cut out," Shakespeare said.

"Why not?"

"Because Buffalo Horn and Running Elk are right. A man must keep his word or he isn't much of a man."

"And you gave your word to marry someone?"

"About twenty years ago."

Nate cradled the Hawken in his arms and scrutinized his friend's tormented countenance. "Why don't you start at the beginning and tell me the whole story? The Flatheads will be busy for a while."

Sighing, Shakespeare stepped to a low boulder and sat down. He placed his rifle stock on the ground and gripped the barrel with both hands, his shoulders slumped in dejection. "You know I was once married to a Flathead called Rainbow Woman."

"You never mentioned her name."

"I don't like to talk about her much. Some memories are just too painful to bring out in the open," Shakespeare said, his voice lowering. "She was the most beautiful woman who ever walked this earth and I loved her with all of my soul."

"The Blackfeet killed her, didn't they?" Nate

brought up, and promptly regretted his stupidity when he saw Shakespeare wince as if from a physical blow.

"Yep. The stinking vermin hit the village one day at dawn. I told her to stay in our lodge while I went out to help the Flathead warriors fight them off." Shakespeare paused, inner pain twisting his face. "But of course she didn't listen. Women never do. She came out with a bow and was covering my back. I didn't even know it until she shouted a warning when a Blackfoot came at me from behind." He stopped and bowed his head, his shaggy mane of hair falling down over his eyes.

"What happened next?" Nate asked.

"I shot the Blackfoot, but while I was taking care of him another of the murdering sons of bitches put an arrow in Rainbow Woman."

Nate made no comment, his heart going out to the profoundly sad man seated in front of him, in perfect sympathy with his friend because he knew all too well how he would feel if the same fate were to befall his precious Winona.

"I left the Flatheads shortly after that terrible day," Shakespeare said.

"But what does all this have to do with Buffalo Horn taking you back for another marriage?" Nate inquired, hoping the change of topic would cheer McNair up.

Shakespeare straightened, the corners of his eyes slightly moist. "Rainbow Woman had two brothers, Buffalo Horn and Spotted Owl. I was good friends with them and spent a lot of time with Spotted Owl. One night, about a year before she was killed, we were sitting in his lodge and got around to discussing what would happen to our wives if either of us ever died. Indian men have a much shorter life expectancy than their women, you see. Well, we didn't want our wives to be forced to fend for themselves, and we damn sure didn't want them to take up with just any warrior who was interested in them so they'd have food to eat and a lodge to live in. So we took a vow."

"A vow?"

"Yes. Spotted Owl promised that if something ever happened to me, he would look after his sister. And I gave my word that if Spotted Owl should die, I would take his wife, Blue Water Woman, into my lodge."

Shakespeare fell silent, and suddenly Nate understood. "Spotted Owl has died?" he probed.

The mountain man nodded. "About six months ago. Buffalo Horn offered to take Blue Water Woman into his lodge, but she insisted that he find me and make me honor my vow."

"What?" Nate said in surprise. "After so many years have gone by since you made the promise? Why?"

"If I knew the answer to that I'd be a happy man," Shakespeare said, his tone conveying sheer misery. "Apparently, Buffalo Horn has been searching for me since then. Then he ran into a trapper from Canada, Frenchy D'Arnot, he's called, and that rascal Frenchy told him exactly where my cabin was. Even drew a map with all the major landmarks." Shakespeare's eyes acquired a flinty cast. "And here I thought Frenchy was a friend. Wait until I get my hands on him."

"If he's a friend, why did he do such a thing?"

"Because Frenchy is the biggest practical joker who ever wore pants. He's always pulling a trick on someone. Giving Buffalo Horn directions to my cabin was his way of having a laugh at my expense."

"Speaking of your cabin, why was it in such a mess?"

Shakespeare brightened somewhat. "Because I was determined not to go with Buffalo Horn and he was determined to take me. It took all ten of them to get me onto my horse."

"So you were never in any real danger?"

The mountain man bestowed a critical glance on his protege. "I keep forgetting that you've only been married a short while."

"So?"

"You still have romance in your blood. All Winona has to do is flutter her eyes and give you a kiss and you think you're on top of the world," Shakespeare said. "You won't begin to appreciate the true nature of marriage until after your first child is born. Then it will sink in."

"You're exaggerating again."

"Think so, do you?" Shakespeare responded, and laughed. "Nate, marriage is the most dangerous fate that can befall a man. Dangerous, because it's also the most glorious, and glorious because our passion overrides our wisdom and transforms us into doting idolaters at the altar of sweet Venus."

"You've lost me. Is that more Shakespeare?"

"No, I'm not quoting old William S. this time. I'm speaking from experience."

"Are you saying that the state of marriage is bad, that all marriages are wrong?"

"Never in a million years. Every man should get married. It's one of the reasons the good Lord put us here. If He had meant for men to be with men, He never would have created women."

"Then what's your point?"

"I'm simply saying that marriage is a heady nectar better sipped than gulped."

Nate shook his head in exasperation. "Do you know what would make *me* a happy man?"

"No. What?"

"Just once I'd like to know what the blazes you're talking about."

The mountain man threw back his head and cackled. Then he stood and slowly walked to the rim. "I reckon I'll have to face her, after all. I'll never be able to live with myself if I don't."

"Do you mean Blue Water Woman?" Nate asked.

Shakespeare nodded. "Running from a problem never does any good. The problem only comes back later, worse than before."

Why, Nate wondered, did he intuitively sense there was more to the situation—something Shakespeare wasn't revealing? He had the feeling his friend was holding back, but he decided to respect his mentor's privacy and not pry.

"You haven't told me," Shakespeare said. "What were you doing at my cabin?"

Nate shrugged. Now wasn't the proper time or place to bring up his own problems. "I was out hunting and wound up in the area."

"Are you pulling my leg?"

"What makes you say that?"

Shakespeare snickered. "Oh, just the fact that there's more game in the Rockies than there are fleas on a mangy mongrel. Still, you couldn't find anything to shoot at in the twenty-five mile stretch of virgin wilderness between your cabin and mine." His eyes narrowed. "Do you reckon I was born yesterday?"

"Of course not," Nate said defensively. He wanted to tell the truth, but he suddenly felt quite silly about bothering his friend over Winona's delivery. Shakespeare had just made fun of his knowledge of the marital state; bringing up the birth would only compound the mountain man's low assessment of his knowledge.

"Suit yourself," Shakespeare said. "Just remember old William S. had a few words to say on the subject."

"He did?"

"This above all; to thine own self be true, and it must follow, as the night the day, thou canst not then be false to any man," Shakespeare quoted.

"I seem to recall you told me that once before," Nate noted.

"Some words of wisdom bear repeating as often as necessary," Shakespeare responded.

"At least I understood you this time," Nate said, slightly miffed. "And I should think it works both ways."

"How's that?"

Nate locked his eyes on his mentor's. "I thought only those without sin are supposed to cast stones."

A look of sheer incredulity rippled over Shakespeare's face, then he laughed. "It's good to see that you know the Bible."

Suddenly, from the gully, arose a tremendous chorus of exultant whoops and screeches.

Gazing down, Nate saw that four of the Utes had been decapitated, their heads impaled on lances, and now the Flatheads were venting their delight while the gory trophies were hoisted high into the air. He noticed blood dripping from one of the heads onto Buffalo Horn's shoulders and felt sick again.

"So noble one minute, so savage the next," Shakespeare commented thoughtfully. "Nature's children are a paradox in themselves."

"Do you want me to go with you to their village?" Nate inquired.

"The choice is yours," Shakespeare replied. "I don't need looking after at my age." He scratched his chin. "And I should think you'd want to return to Winona as soon as possible. She's well along in the family way, as I recollect."

"In two moons the baby is due."

"Then you'd better skedaddle for your cabin or she'll greet you with a pan in her hand."

"What about you?"

"I'll be fine," Shakespeare said. "I haven't gotten all these white hairs by being careless."

Nate smiled, but his emotions were in turmoil. By all rights he should return to Winona immediately, yet he didn't want to simply ride off and leave Shakespeare, to abandon his friend at a time when Shakespeare might need him to be around. He owed the old-timer more than he could ever hope to repay, and here was an opportunity, however slight, to make good on part of the debt.

The barbaric celebration in the gully took over five minutes to wind down. Only a few Flatheads were still cutting Utes to pieces when Buffalo Horn and Running Elk mounted their horses and rode up the trail to the top.

"Shakespeare, my friend!" Buffalo Horn declared as he jumped to the ground. "You are as clever as a fox and as dangerous as the wolverine you are named after." He walked up to the mountain man and slapped McNair on the back. "Our people will hold a great celebration a few days after we return to honor this victory."

"Glad I could help," Shakespeare said.

Running Elk, still on his horse, vented a triumphant shriek, then said, "I am glad I lived to see this day. Utes killed my brother years ago, and now I have avenged his death." He looked at McNair. "Did you deliberately lead the band into the gully?"

"Yes," Shakespeare said. "I remembered being in this neck of the woods some time back, beaver hunting. I knew about the opening in the wall and figured we could stop them cold."

"As usual, your judgment has won the day,"

Buffalo Horn said. His eyes drifted to the mountain man's weapons and he frowned. "But now we have another matter to talk about. Will you agree to come with us or not? If so, we won't try to take your guns from you or tie you onto your horse. If not, then everything is as before."

Shakespeare expelled a long breath, then nodded. "I've thought it over and decided to go to the village and settle this personally."

Buffalo Horn beamed. "You have made my heart happy." He turned to Nate. "And what of you, Grizzly Killer? Will you come with us also?"

Nate became aware of Shakespeare's eyes boring into him. He deliberately ignored him and asked, "How far is it to your village?"

"We will be there by late tomorrow afternoon," Buffalo Horn disclosed.

Just one more day. Nate felt a twinge of guilt in the depths of his conscience as he forced his lips to form his next words. "Yes, I'll tag along if you don't mind."

"You are more than welcome," Buffalo Horn said. "My people will greet you with open arms."

Nate gazed down at his moccasins, thinking *I just hope Winona does the same when I get back to our cabin.* He gripped the Hawken in his left hand, studiously avoided looking at Shakespeare, and walked to his stallion.

Chapter Seven

The Flathead village was nestled in a picturesque valley at the juncture of Beaverhead Creek and Stinking Creek, as they were known. Composed of 180 lodges stretched out on the south side of the junction, the village teemed with life; warriors working on their weapons, engaged in games of chance or conducting horse races; women curing buffalo hides, doing bead work or cooking; and children everywhere, playing and laughing in delighted abandon.

Nate first surveyed the sprawling village from the crest of a hill to the southwest. Buffalo Horn and Running Elk led the warriors, eager to see their loved ones again, down the slope at a canter. He was with Shakespeare, bringing up the rear.

"How times do change," the mountain man remarked philosophically.

"Why do you say that?" Nate asked.

Shakespeare nodded at the village. "When I lived among the Flatheads, things were a lot different. In the summer they lived in lodges consisting of cottonwood frames covered with thick bullrush mats. In the winter they lived in earth houses that were partly underground." He sighed. "Then they started trading with the fur companies and with other tribes. They took to imitating the tribes east of the Rockies, living like the Blackfeet and the Cheyenne. Now you can hardly tell the difference."

"Is that so bad?" Nate inquired in mild surprise. He'd grown to admire certain aspects of the Indian way of life quite highly, including their rugged independence, their appreciation of Nature, their close-knit families, and, in the case of tribes like the Flatheads and Shoshones, their innate friendliness.

"No, I reckon not," Shakespeare said. "At least the Flatheads never got around to flattening heads like some of the tribes off to the northwest do."

Nate wasn't certain he'd heard correctly. "Flattening heads? Are you telling another tall tale?"

"This is plain fact," Shakespeare said. "Tribes that live out near the Pacific Ocean have this custom of flattening the heads of their babies by tying a board over the skull until it becomes the right shape."

"Why in the world would they want to do that?"

"I guess they figure it makes them more attractive. Some even pierce their noses and stick small bones and rings in the holes."

"Now I know you're pulling my leg."

Shakespeare snorted in indignation. "Ignorance and blindfolds have a lot in common." He looked at Nate. "Have you ever been to the Pacific Ocean?"

"You know I haven't."

"Then until you do, don't go around implying that someone who has is a liar."

"I didn't mean to offend you," Nate said, not knowing what to make of his friend's unusual testy behavior.

The corners of Shakespeare's mouth curled down

and he turned his head to gaze to the west. "No, I suppose you didn't. Sorry."

Nate rode in silence to the bottom of the hill. Already Buffalo Horn and the rest were dozens of yards ahead. He studied the people in the village for a moment, then said, "There's something I don't understand. These Indians have heads shaped just like ours, normal in every respect. So why are they called Flatheads if they don't flatten their heads?"

Shakespeare chuckled. "Observant cuss, aren't you?" He reached up and tapped his brow. "Yes, the Flatheads have normal heads. They have flat foreheads just like ours, not peaked ones like the tribes I was telling you about."

"Why would anyone call a tribe with normal heads the Flatheads? Shouldn't it be the other way around?"

"You'd think so," Shakespeare said. "Blame the French for the confusion. It was some of their early trappers who got the names all backwards."

Nate laughed lightly. His mentor's store of knowledge never ceased to amaze him, and he wondered if he would ever be as wise in the ways of the people and wildlife of the Rockies as was Shakespeare.

The return of Buffalo Horn's party had caused a widespread stir in the village. People were coming from all directions, the warriors dressed in buckskin shirts, pants, and moccasins, the women in beaded dresses. Buffalo Horn and the other returning braves were relating their adventures to groups of intent listeners.

Nate noticed Shakespeare craning his neck to scan the crowd. "Do you see her yet?" he asked.

"Who?"

"Lady Godiva."

"I'm not looking for anyone special."

"If you say so," Nate said dryly. He saw many Flatheads turning to regard Shakespeare and him with intense interest, and he straightened in the saddle and held his Hawken firmly across his thighs. When Shakespeare reined up a moment later, he did the same.

A number of tribe members detached themselves from different groups and came over to the mountain man. Cheerful greetings were exchanged, and Shakespeare dismounted to give several warm bear hugs.

Nate listened to their conversation, conducted in the Flathead tongue, and wished he spoke the language. He felt a bit like a bump on a log. A few smiles were displayed his way, but no one stepped forward to talk to him until a young warrior boldly moved up to his side and addressed him in the Flathead language. He shook his head and used his hands to reply in sign language, "I am sorry. I do not know your tongue."

The warrior grinned, his own fingers flying as he said, "And I do not know yours. I am Wind In The Grass."

"I am called Grizzly Killer," Nate signed.

Wind In The Grass cocked his head to one side. "The same one who helped the Shoshones defeat Mad Dog?"

"Yes," Nate responded, slightly embarrassed by his notoriety. Bitter memories of the conflict between his adopted tribe and Mad Dog, a brutal Blackfoot who had led a war party in a raid into Shoshone territory, filtered through his mind. Winona's father and mother had lost their lives during the deciding battle that resulted in Mad Dog's death and a bloody, costly victory over the Blackfeet.

"I heard about you from some white trappers who stopped at our village," Wind In The Grass revealed.

"Some men talk too much," Nate signed, grinning.

Wind In The Grass smiled. "I would be honored if you would stay with my family while you are here."

Nate glanced at Shakespeare, who was busily greeting old friends, unsure of what to do. He knew to refuse such unselfish hospitality would be construed as an insult, and he certainly didn't want to offend anyone, in addition to which, sleeping in a lodge was vastly preferable to sleeping on the hard ground. "I will be happy to stay with you," he responded.

"Good," Wind In The Grass signed, and motioned northward. "Come, and I will show you where my lodge is."

Dismounting, Nate held the stallion's reins in one hand, his rifle in the other, and walked alongside his new acquaintance, threading among the Flatheads and the teepees until they came to a small lodge not far from Stinking Creek. Only twelve feet high and patched in two spots with newer pieces of hide, the plain dwelling indicated an important fact to Nate: His friendly host was a poor man. Just as in white society, there were wealthy and poverty-stricken Indians. The lodge of a well-to-do warrior might be fifteen to twenty feet high, the hides would be in perfect condition, and the exterior would be gaily adorned with symbols important to the owner.

For confirmation of his hunch, Nate had only to gaze at the four horses grazing nearby. Three were mares well past their prime. The fourth was a stallion that also showed its age and undoubtedly served as Wind In The Grass's war and buffalo mount. Since a warrior's prowess could be measured by the number of animals he had stolen from other tribes, it meant that Wind In The Grass had yet to fully prove himself.

The flap to the lodge was down. Wind In The Grass turned to Nate and signed, "Wait here while I tell my wife the news." He went inside.

Nate became aware of other Flatheads staring at him and did his best to stand in a dignified but appropriately humble manner. Suddenly, from within, arose loud voices, that of a woman and Wind In The Grass arguing heatedly. He suspected the wife was objecting to his surprise stay and debated whether to simply walk off. But to do so would greatly humiliate Wind In The Grass. He decided to wait and see if the warrior would change his mind about the offer.

A second later the flap opened and a sheepish Wind In The Grass signed, "Come in, Grizzly Killer. My wife is very pleased that our lodge will be honored with your presence."

Feeling uncomfortable, Nate ground-hitched the stallion and entered, racking his brain to recall the lodge etiquette rules Shakespeare had previously imparted to him. He remembered that when a male visitor entered a lodge, he should always step to the right and wait for the owner to seat him. So he promptly did so, his eyes adjusting to the reduced illumination.

Standing beside a buffalo paunch cooking pot situated in the center of the teepee, directly under the ventilation opening at the top, was a skinny young woman with long dark hair and a pointed nose. She mustered a wan smile and gave a deferential bow.

"Grizzly Killer, this is Flower Woman," Wind In The Grass introduced his wife.

"I am happy to meet you," Nate signed, the Hawken tucked in the crook of his left arm. He heard a peculiar cooing noise and glanced to his right to find a baby in a cradle board that was propped against the lodge wall. Most Indian tribes used such devices in one form or another. Consisting of a skin pouch laced around a wooden frame, the cradleboard constituted an infant's tiny home until the child was capable of walking. Every tribe had a different style that was typically used, and in this instance the cradleboard flared out at the top to provide a soft leather cushion for the child's head to rest on. He noticed the outer skin had been artistically decorated with elaborate bead work.

Wind In The Grass walked over to the cradleboard and gestured proudly. "This is my son, Roaring Mountain, who will one day grow up to be a mighty warrior in the Flathead nation."

"I am certain he will," Nate signed, and looked at the wife. "The cradleboard you made is one of the nicest I have ever seen," he complimented her, not bothering to mention that he'd only viewed two or three up close during his brief time in the Rockies. His statement had the desired effect.

Flower Woman beamed happily and moved her thin fingers in a grateful answer. "Thank you. I worked very hard to give our son the best cradleboard I could."

Nate gave the cradleboard another appreciative appraisal. "Such a fine cradleboard is worth saving for your son's children to use. They will remember your kindness always."

"I had not thought of that," Flower Woman replied, even more pleased. "It is a good idea."

"Where are my manners?" Wind In The Grass signed, and motioned for Nate to take the seat of honor located to the rear of the cooking fire and to the left of the spot where the warrior would himself sit. "You must want to rest after so much riding."

"We did come a long way," Nate noted, and walked to the proper spot. He sank down with a sigh, sitting cross-legged as warriors customarily did. Women, however, were prohibited from ever doing so. Any female who did was branded as possessing lax morals. "And that fight with the Utes did tire me out a bit."

"I heard Running Elk speak of it," Wind In The

Grass mentioned. "In a few days there will be a celebration and all the warriors who took part will tell of the battle." He paused. "But we would enjoy hearing your story now, if you wish."

Nate obliged, giving them a brief account of the chase and the battle in the gully. By the time he was done his arms were tired. He noticed that Wind In The Grass hung on every sign and detected an enthusiastic gleam in the young warrior's eyes, leading him to suspect that his host had been in very few life or death conflicts. If he was right, Wind In The Grass couldn't wait to prove himself on a raid and earn the respect of the entire tribe.

At the conclusion of the report, Flower Woman devoted herself to the meal she had been preparing before their arrival. She walked to a rawhide parfleche, one of several artistically decorated carrying bags lying against the south side, and removed a handful of wild onions.

"We are having buffalo stew tonight," Wind In The Grass signed. "I hope that will be all right."

"I enjoy stew," Nate assured him. He observed Flower Woman pause, then reach into the parfleche for more onions. They must have meager food stores, he deduced, and decided to eat sparingly but praise her cooking to high heaven. As he watched her chop the onions into pieces, he reflected that coming to the village had been a bad idea. Shakespeare obviously didn't need him around. Tomorrow morning, first thing, he would head for home.

A patter of rushing footsteps sounded outside, and suddenly a voice called out urgently in the Flathead language.

Wind In The Grass promptly answered, and in poked the head of another young warrior who immediately launched into an excited narrative. Wind In

The Grass then turned in alarm to Nate and signed, "You should go to Carcajou right away."

"What is wrong?" Nate asked, beginning to rise, trying to guess what sort of trouble Shakespeare could have gotten into in such a short time in a village where he obviously had a great many friends. The answer was totally unexpected.

"He is fighting one of our warriors."

Chapter Eight

Nate raced out of the lodge with his rifle in hand. Without a word the young warrior who had brought the report turned and raced to the south, and Nate sped along on his flying heels. Behind him came Wind In The Grass. Apparently news of the fight was spreading rapidly because there were other Flatheads hastening in the same direction.

He heard the commotion moments before he saw it, heard men and women shouting and children shrieking in their high-pitched voices, and then he rounded a lodge to discover a wide circle of boisterous Flatheads surroundings two grappling figures in the center. The crowd was already three and four deep. In his concern for Shakespeare's safety he didn't bother with polite niceties; instead of requesting those blocking his path to move aside he simply barreled into them and shoved his way through with his broad shoulders.

Nate glimpsed faces registering surprise turning his way. One warrior barked an angry exclamation. In moments he was on the inside, and before him were the struggling combatants.

Shakespeare and a prodigiously muscled warrior were wrestling furiously, rolling over and over, each striving to get the better hold, each red in the face from his strenuous exertions.

Nate looked around. Off to the right stood Buffalo Horn and Running Elk, both apprehensively watching the contest. Off to the left were three warriors Nate didn't know, one a burly Flathead whose features were twisted in a perpetual scowl. Even as he laid eyes on them, they closed in on the fighters.

Buffalo Horn shouted something in his own tongue.

The burly warrior snapped an answer and gestured, as if telling Buffalo Horn to mind his own business.

Confusion gripped Nate. He had no idea what had started the fight, and he didn't know if the threesome approaching his mentor were friends or foes. For all he knew, they were allies of the Indian Shakespeare was battling.

In a swirl of motion the elderly mountain man wound up on top of his adversary, pinning the Flathead's shoulders to the ground with his knees and holding the warrior's hands flat on the grass.

Suddenly the trio darted forward and two of them seized McNair from behind, hauling him off the pinned warrior.

Nate had witnessed enough. He wasn't about to let them or anyone else manhandle his friend. In four bounds he was there, swinging the stock of the Hawken up and around and clipping one of the men holding Shakespeare on the temple. The man fell on the spot.

Bellowing angrily, the burly warrior leaped with outstretched arms.

Nate pivoted, rammed the rifle's heavy barrel into

the Flathead's stomach, doubling him over, then whipped the stock into the wheezing warrior's forehead, dropping him also.

The third Flathead let go of McNair and sprang, his left hand grasping Nate's shoulder.

All it took was a slight twist and Nate buried the stock in the man's abdomen. The warrior staggered backwards, sputtering. Out of the corner of his right eye Nate saw the muscular Flathead on the ground going for a hip knife, and he instantly swung around to train the Hawken on the man's forehead as his thumb pulled the hammer back with an audible click. He touched the trigger, his every nerve on edge, ready to fire if the Flathead drew the blade.

Several things happened then.

The warrior froze, his hand just touching the hilt, his dark eyes burning with rage.

A hush promptly descended on the assembled Flatheads. Many gasped.

And Shakespeare took a frantic step forward to grasp the rifle barrel and pull it upward. "Don't shoot!" he cried.

Nate glanced at his friend, then at the ring of Indians. Most were staring at him in nonplused amazement, a few in outright resentment of his interference. He slowly lowered the gun and eased the hammer down.

Buffalo Horn and Running Elk came running over as the muscular warrior stood. From the throng walked a stately individual with gray hair who carried a war club and wore a buckskin shirt on which had been drawn the likeness of a large bird of prey.

Shakespeare rubbed his left side, his hard gaze on his opponent. "Thanks for the assist, Nate, but you shouldn't have interfered. This was between Standing Bear and myself."

"Do you mind telling me what's going on?" Nate requested.

"In a bit," Shakespeare responded, and nodded at the approaching gray-haired warrior. "We might be in for it now. That's White Eagle, their chief. If he's mad, there's no telling what will happen. Whatever he says is law. The Flatheads put more stock in their chiefs than most tribes, and obey their every word."

Stepping back so he could cover Standing Bear and the three he had struck in case they turned hostile, Nate glanced at the stately warrior just as the man reached them.

If ever there was a face that reflected wisdom, this was it. White Eagle held himself with dignity, his severely weathered visage and penetrating eyes reflecting the soul of a man of vast experience. He betrayed neither anger nor condemnation as he looked at each of them in turn, his gaze lingering on Nate, and finally settled on Buffalo Horn. In softly spoken words he addressed the tall Flathead in their mutual language.

A lengthy conversation ensued, with all the Indians in the middle of the circle participating. Standing Bear growled his words and motioned angrily at Shakespeare and Nate. The three Nate had bested chimed in with harsh statements of their own. Finally Shakespeare interjected comments that caused White Eagle to grunt and nod knowingly.

Nate waited impatiently for an explanation. As near as he could tell, Buffalo Horn and Running Elk had sided with Shakespeare in the dispute. Standing Bear seemed to be trying to convince the chief to take some sort of action, but White Eagle evidently refused. After a heated argument, Standing Bear stalked off with the three other warriors in tow.

White Eagle then talked to Shakespeare for several minutes. When they were done the chief smiled, then turned to survey the tribe. He gave a short speech that started the crowd to murmuring, and walked off.

"*Now* will you tell me what's going on?" Nate asked. He saw the people beginning to disperse, conversing in hushed tones with repeated glances at McNair.

"I reckon I should," Shakespeare said.

Buffalo Horn frowned and shook his head. "This is bad, very bad. There will be blood shed before too long and it might well be yours, old friend."

"I'll watch out for myself," Shakespeare promised.

Running Elk made a clucking sound of disapproval. "This is all her fault. She should tell Standing Bear she wants nothing to do with him and there would be no problem."

Shakespeare started slapping dust and bits of grass from his buckskins. "She has her reasons, no doubt."

"Perhaps," Buffalo Horn said, "but I want you to know that I had no idea this would take place. I did not know Standing Bear had an interest in her. Had I, I would never have let her convince me to bring you to our village."

"I understand," Shakespeare said.

Nate's patience had reached its limit. He stepped forward and demanded in an irate tone, "Tell me what the blazes is going on."

"Oh. Sorry," Shakespeare said, continuing to dust himself off. He paused to stare after Standing Bear. "It seems I have a rival for Blue Water Woman's affection."

"The two of you were fighting over her?" Nate asked in astonishment. He found the notion of someone Shakespeare's age brawling over a woman almost ridiculous.

Shakespeare nodded. "Sort of. One minute I was talking to several old friends and the next Standing

Bear walked up and demanded to know if it was true that I intended to take Blue Water Woman for my wife."

"What did you tell him?"

"I said it was more like the other way around. He informed me that she was going to be his wife, no one else's, and gave me a shove to emphasize his point."

"And you shoved back."

"Naturally. So we wound up rolling around in the grass until you arrived and turned a minor disagreement into a life or death dispute," Shakespeare said. Neither his eyes or his tone betrayed any hint of reproach.

"I didn't mean to," Nate said, aware the two Flatheads were regarding him critically. "I thought you were in trouble."

"I know," Shakespeare said, and chuckled. "I must admit you handled them better than I could have done myself."

"It is not funny," Buffalo Horn interjected. "Now Standing Bear, Bad Face, Smoke, and Wolf Ribs have been insulted. They will try to restore their honor by humiliating Nate as badly as they were shamed."

Running Elk nodded. "In front of the entire tribe, no less." He focused on Nate. "I know those men well. They are not the kind to forgive and forget, particularly Bad Face. You must be on your guard here every minute."

Nate didn't need to ask which one of the threesome had been Bad Face. It had to be the burly warrior with the perpetual scowl.

Shakespeare placed a friendly hand on Nate's shoulder. "I know you meant well, son, but you've put yourself in a dangerous situation. The best thing for you to do would be to mount up at dawn and head for your cabin."

"You want me to run?" Nate inquired in disbelief.

"I wouldn't put it in those words," Shakespeare said.

"It sounds like running to me," Nate declared. "And I'm not about to let Bad Face and the rest think I'm a yellow belly."

"The wise man knows when to fight and when to make tracks, and knows the difference between causes worth fighting for and those that are just a matter of personal pride."

"Are you leaving?"

"I can't."

"Then neither am I."

The mountain man was clearly displeased. He walked a few yards to the west and leaned down to retrieve his Hawken, which was lying in the grass, then straightened. "How about if I ask you to leave as a personal favor to me?"

"Ask me anything else and I'd do it," Nate said. "But I'm not about to turn tail for you or anyone else." He was peeved his friend would even suggest such a degrading act. During his long trip out from St. Louis with his Uncle Zeke, he'd learned the hard way that in the wilderness a man was invariably measured by the bravery he exhibited. Cowards were generally disdained by whites and Indians alike. Several tribes went so far as to force men who had attained a certain age and still not displayed the courage expected of them by counting coup or stealing horses to perform the jobs of women. The Crows, in fact, made such men the slaves of the women; they were compelled to obey every order a woman gave, to carry wood, fetch water, and do every menial job imaginable. It was widely known that braves who fell into the ranks of the women became supremely eager to prove themselves and thus overcome the terrible stigma.

Shakespeare gave him a strange look. "No, I guess you're not. Very well. We'll just have to wait for them to make the next move." He paused. "I apologize for not paying much attention to you when we arrived. I had other things on my mind."

"I know."

McNair smiled. "Now we need to find you a place to stay. I've been invited to hang my moccasins in Buffalo Horn's lodge. Maybe Running Elk would—."

"I already have somewhere to stay," Nate interrupted.

"You do? Where?"

Before Nate could reply, Wind In The Grass stepped forward and rather nervously said "With me, Carcajou. I invited Grizzly Killer to share my lodge for as long as he is in our village."

Nate noticed both Buffalo Horn and Running Elk frown as if severely displeased by the disclosure.

"Do I know you?" Shakespeare said in return.

"I am Wind In The Grass," the young warrior revealed. "I was only two years old when last you were in our village, or so I was once told by my father. You knew him well, I believe."

"Who is he?" Shakespeare inquired.

"Little Hawk."

The mountain man grinned. "Yes, indeed. He and I go back a long ways. Where is he? I would like to see him again."

"The Blackfeet killed him," Wind In The Grass said slowly.

"Oh. Sorry to hear it. Your father was a good man, a brave warrior."

Buffalo Horn nodded, then said, "In truth he was. Now if only his son would demonstrate the same courage, it would make everyone in the tribe very happy."

"What are you talking about?" Nate inquired.

"It is best for Wind In The Grass to tell you himself," Buffalo Horn answered.

"Yes, if he can stand the shame," added Running Elk.

Nate glanced at his host and detected the hurt in his eyes. He felt the two older warriors were being unduly harsh and determined to get to the bottom of it later, when Wind In The Grass could relate the details in private. For now there was a much more important matter to discuss. "I'll be glad to hear the details some other time," he said, turning to Shakespeare. "I'm more interested in hearing what you plan to do about this contrary female who might wind up getting you killed."

"Perhaps it would help if we got her side of the story," Shakespeare suggested.

"When?" Nate asked, eager to get the matter settled so he could return to Winona.

"Right now, if you want," Shakespeare said, and gazed over Nate's shoulder. "She's standing right behind you."

Chapter Nine

Nate had seldom been as embarrassed as he was at that very moment. He hesitated before turning, trying to compose his face so he wouldn't betray his feelings. Then he slowly pivoted, not knowing what to expect but certainly not expecting the sight that befell his surprised gaze.

Blue Water Woman stood three feet away, attired in a beautiful beaded dress that barely did her justice. Raven hair fell to the small of her back, framing an oval face remarkable for its smooth complexion and deep, dark eyes. Her lips were full, her nostrils thin. Her teeth, when she smiled, were small and white.

"Hello," Nate blurted, and mentally berated himself for being an idiot. She might not even speak English. He had to admit she was one of the loveliest woman he'd ever seen, perhaps even second to Winona. She betrayed no sign of her age, yet he knew she must be nearly as old as Shakespeare.

"Hello, Grizzly Killer," she replied, her pronunciation crisp and precise. "This contrary female is very pleased to meet the famous man she had heard so much about."

Nate wished he could shrivel up like a dry plant and disappear. Either that, or beat his head against a tree. He mustered the friendliest smile of which he was capable and said, "You must be Blue Water Woman. I've heard a lot about you, too."

"Have you, now?" she responded, and looked at McNair.

"He thinks he has," Shakespeare said quickly, "but he doesn't know the bare bones."

Blue Water Woman nodded. "That is nice to hear." She held out her right hand toward Nate. "I believe this is the customary way whites greet each other."

"Sure is," Nate said, shaking. He got the impression there had been a hidden meaning to his mentor's words, but for the life of him he couldn't figure out what it might be. "I'm pleased to make your acquaintance."

Buffalo Horn stepped forward. "Did you see the fight between Carcajou and Standing Bear?" he asked angrily.

"I saw," Blue Water Woman answered, letting go of Nate's hand.

"What do you have to say for yourself?" Buffalo Horn demanded.

"I have no control over Standing Bear," she said.

"Did you know he was interested in you before you begged me to go after Shakespeare?"

"Yes," Blue Water Woman stated calmly, then added, "And I did not *beg* you to go find Shakespeare. I asked you."

The tall Flathead's features became iron. "And you did not think to warn me so I could warn him?"

Blue Water Woman refused to be intimidated. She

replied in an even tone, "I have told Standing Bear many times that I have no interest in sharing his lodge. He refuses to accept me at my word."

"Has he courted you?"

"He sent Wolf Ribs with four fine horses. I sent them back. He also sent Smoke over with a deer he had killed, but I sent it back, too."

"This is bad," Running Elk commented.

"I will tell you what my heart feels," Buffalo Horn said to Blue Water Woman. "I believe you deliberately did not tell me because you knew I would not want to involve my brother Shakespeare in a fight with Standing Bear. I believe you deceived me."

Blue Water Woman stiffened indignantly. "I have never deceived you in all the years we have known each other. I did not expect Standing Bear to challenge Carcajou."

"Before this is over, there might be blood spilled," Buffalo Horn said. "And it will be on your shoulders." He turned on his heels and walked off, Running Elk dogging his heels.

Nate detected profound sadness in the woman's eyes and felt sorry for her. He suddenly realized that Shakespeare would probably like to be alone with her and turned. "Well, I'd better be getting along myself."

"I'll look you up later," Shakespeare said, his eyes on Blue Water Woman.

"No rush," Nate said, heading northward. Wind In The Grass fell in beside him. He glanced back once to see his friend holding her hand. Neither was saying a word; they simply stood and stared into each other's eyes. And here he thought Shakespeare had been upset with her.

They walked for a dozen yards when Wind In The Grass turned and asked in sign, "How did you learn to be so brave?"

"I'm no braver than most," Nate replied absently, still thinking about Shakespeare and the strange manner in which his mentor had been behaving.

"That is not true," Wind In The Grass said. "I was there. I saw you go up against the four worst men in our village, and you never hesitated." He laughed lightly. "You beat all of them in the time it takes to blink."

"You take after the Wolverine," Nate signed. "Both of you exaggerate stories."

"This is a very serious matter to me," Wind In The Grass noted. "I would not make light of it."

"I did not mean to insult you," Nate signed.

Wind In The Grass sighed and gazed toward Stinking Creek. "Did you see the way the older warriors treated me?"

"What do you mean?" Nate responded, feigning innocence.

"Buffalo Horn and Running Elk do not think I am much of a man. Many other men in our tribe feel the same way."

"Do they have a reason?"

"They think they do," Wind In The Grass signed.

"Want to talk about it?" Nate inquired, certain the young warrior had broached the subject for that very reason.

"If you do not mind."

"Why would I mind? Go ahead."

Wind In The Grass moved his arms and fingers in a fluid flow. "It all started eight moons ago when I took part in a raid on a Blackfoot village. It was the first such raid I had been on. Buffalo Horn was in charge, and he left me in a gully to watch the horses while he and the others snuck up on the Blackfeet. All went well at first. They gathered nine Blackfoot animals and started back to where I waited." He stopped, his expression forlorn.

"What happened next?" Nate prompted.

"I was sitting there on my horse when three Blackfeet came out of nowhere. They had been off hunting because one had a small antelope slung over his shoulder. Two had bows, one a rifle. The moment they saw me they shouted and charged. I put an arrow in the first one, then the brave with the rifle fired." He lowered his arms for a moment. "The shot missed me but scared several of the horses and they bolted along the gully. The rest followed. I had a choice to make. Either I could stay and fight the two Blackfeet, who had taken cover, or I could go after the horses and retrieve them so my friends could make their escape. I went after the horses."

Nate nodded. "I think I would have done the same," he signed.

"Thank you," Wind In The Grass said. "But there is more. The Blackfeet in the village heard the shot and rushed out to investigate. They spied Buffalo Horn and the others and gave chase, forcing our warriors to let go of the horses they had stolen. Buffalo Horn led our warriors to the gully, but I was not there. They took shelter in nearby woods and fought a running battle for many miles before the Blackfeet turned around and returned to their village. Two of our warriors were killed."

"And they blame you?"

"I gathered the horses as quickly as I could, but they had scattered over several miles," Wind In The Grass related. "By the time I tracked Buffalo Horn and the rest down, they were far into the forest. Some of them accused me of running off. I explained about the three Blackfeet, but it seemed to make little difference."

"Surely Buffalo Horn saw the two Blackfeet who were still in the gully when you rode off?"

"No," Wind In The Grass signed. "The pair must have seen our warriors coming and hid, or else they had gone after me and were not there when Buffalo Horn and the others got back."

Nate pursed his lips, pondering the tale. Small wonder that Buffalo Horn and Running Elk had treated his host so coldly. Wind In The Grass bore the worst stigma any Indian warrior could ever have; that of being a coward. The young warrior was branded unless he could prove them all wrong.

Wind In The Grass cleared his throat. "I will understand if you want to move out of our lodge and stay with someone else."

The poor man practically radiated anguish, and Nate wasn't about to add insult to injury. "Are you throwing me out?" he signed.

"No, of course not," Wind In The Grass replied. "I just—."

"Then why bring it up?" Nate cut him off. "I certainly do not believe you ran away on purpose."

Wind In The Grass looked at him. "You do not?"

"I always take a man at his word unless he gives me cause to think otherwise," Nate explained. "And I think I know you well enough to say that you are the kind of man who would stick by his friends through the worst possible danger. You are definitely not a coward." He smiled, hoping his words had cheered the warrior up. To his astonishment, tears welled in the man's eyes.

"Thank you, Grizzly Killer," Wind In The Grass signed.

"Be patient," Nate advised. "You will get your chance to prove yourself to their satisfaction." He chuckled. "In a way, you remind me of myself a year ago."

"I do?"

"Yes. I had a lot to prove when I first came to the wilderness. If it had not been for a grizzly that tried to take its own life by throwing itself on my knife, I still might have a lot to prove."

Wind In The Grass tossed back his head and laughed in delight. "Thank you for those kind words," he then signed. "But I may not be able to prove myself if no one will take me on a raid."

"No one?"

"Buffalo Horn has been out twice since that terrible time. Running Elk and several others have also led raids against different enemies. None have invited me along, and no one will go with me should I try to lead one."

The man had a problem, Nate reflected. Wind In The Grass needed witnesses when he demonstrated his bravery to refute those who accused him of cowardice. But if none of the other warriors would associate with him, Wind In The Grass had no way of clearing his reputation.

Suddenly, from their rear, a gruff voice barked out a string of words in the Flathead tongue.

Nate turned, and was shocked to see his four newly made enemies advancing toward him. They were still a dozen feet off. He raised the Hawken, covering them, and they immediately halted.

Standing Bear addressed Wind In The Grass, who gave a brief answer. The muscular warrior grunted, then resorted to sign. "This coward tells me you are fluent in sign language."

Other Flatheads had stopped their activities to view the confrontation, including two gawking boys nearby.

Averse to lowering the rifle, Nate nonetheless did. He couldn't use sign with his hands full, and he wasn't about to let the quartet think he was afraid of them. After tucking the Hawken in the crook of his left elbow, he glared at them and replied, "Call my friend a coward again and we will finish what you started earlier."

Bad Face hissed and made as if to attack, but a word from Standing Bear froze him in place.

"We have no quarrel with you, Grizzly Killer," the muscular warrior signed. "I came to apologize for what happened."

Surprise delayed Nate's response. Could it be he had misjudged Standing Bear's character? No, he doubted it. Still, he had to exercise proper Indian protocol. "Your apology is accepted."

"I also want you to talk to Carcajou," Standing Bear said.

"About what?"

"Tell him to leave our village at first light. Tell him Blue Water Woman is going to be my woman and no one else's. Tell him no one will take her from me."

Nate felt his temper flare. The gall of the man, he mused, and signed emphatically, "Tell him yourself unless *you* are a coward."

Standing Bear took a pace forward, his hand straying toward his knife. He glanced at the Hawken and the pistols, scowled, and dropped the notion. "I can see words are wasted on you. You are as stubborn as your friend, Carcajou. It will be fitting for the two of you to die together."

"A lot of men have tried to kill us," Nate signed "and their corpses are feeding the worms."

The muscular warrior snorted. "How did a cub like you ever get the name Grizzly Killer?"

"The hard way," Nate replied. "How is it the four of you are strutting around like men when you should be mending hides with the women?"

Again Bad Face made as if to leap. The other two grabbed his arms and held him fast.

"This is not the end of it," Standing Bear signed.

"You will regret the day you insulted us." Wheeling, he stalked off with his three friends in tow. Bad Face kept glancing back and glaring.

Nate heard Wind In The Grass expel a long breath. He cradled the Hawken and resumed walking toward his host's lodge. "Now what were we discussing?"

"Bravery," the warrior answered. "And I will tell you here and now that you are either the bravest man I have ever met, or else the biggest fool who ever lived. Those men will not rest until you are dead."

"Then maybe I should move out of your lodge. It might be safer for your family."

"Nonsense. You may stay as long as you want. Your enemies are my enemies."

They looked at each other, and a genuine friendship was born.

Chapter Ten

Nate awoke before sunrise and glanced at the peacefully slumbering family on the other side of the small lodge. Wind In The Grass snored lightly, while Flower Woman and Roaring Mountain were both breathing deeply. The parents were a foot apart, each with a hand resting on the other, while snugly nestled between them was the infant. He smiled, thinking of Winona and the addition they would have to their own family in a relatively short time, and imagined them sleeping in the same intimate fashion. It warmed his heart.

He slid out from under his blanket, wedged both flintlocks under his belt, and stepped outside for some fresh air, leaving the Hawken by his bedding. As he straightened he was shocked to see his mentor seated cross-legged not six feet away, facing the lodge. To the east a pale rosy light indicated the sun would soon peek above the horizon.

"Good morning," Shakespeare said quietly.

Nate walked over and squatted. "What are you

doing here so early? Is something wrong?"

"Terribly wrong," Shakespeare said, and gazed eastward, his features reflecting fatigue and a strange melancholy.

"What is it?" Nate asked, certain Standing Bear must be somehow involved. "Were you attacked?"

Shakespeare looked at him and grinned. "Not in the way you think. I came here to talk to you. I've been up all night wrestling with a personal problem, and I thought I'd ask your advice.

"*You* want *my* advice?"

"What's so unusual about that?"

"Nothing," Nate said struggling to prevent his amazement from showing. He regarded Shakespeare as the wisest man he'd ever known, as someone capable of handling anything and everything that came along; supremely self-confident and self-reliant. The notion that Shakespeare needed help with a problem was incredible.

"I spent most of the night with Blue Water Woman," Shakespeare disclosed. "We walked and talked about the old days, about how it was when I lived among the Flatheads." He paused. "They were fine times."

"I gather you're not mad at her."

"Mad?" Shakespeare repeated, and snorted. "Nate, I think I'm in love with the woman, just like before."

"Before?" Nate said, bewildered. He promptly sat down, stunned. This made two astounding revelations in a row, and he didn't feel he was alert enough to handle them. He shook his head, dispelling lingering tendrils of sleep from his mind.

"I reckon I should start at the beginning," Shakespeare said, bowing his head.

"Whatever is best," Nate replied, hearing a camp dog yip to the west.

"It all began before I even met Rainbow Woman," Shakespeare said, "and before Blue Water Woman was married to Spotted Owl. We knew each other. In fact, we were quite fond of one another. I made every excuse I could to see her, and we talked about maybe becoming man and wife one day."

"But you wound up marrying Rainbow Woman instead?" Nate asked in confusion.

"Let me explain," Shakespeare said. "You see, Blue Water Woman's father didn't like me. I suspect he was a bigoted son of a bitch who didn't like whites, period. So when our romance became serious and we started to think about living together, he put his foot down and forbade me to see her."

"Did you stop?"

Inner pain was briefly visible on the mountain man's weathered countenance. "Yes. Only because I had no choice. Indian culture is a lot different from ours in some respects. It's unthinkable, for instance, for a young woman to go against her father's wishes. His word was law."

"So you went your separate ways?"

Shakespeare nodded slowly. "I don't mind admitting I was half out of my mind with grief. I even climbed a cliff, figuring I would throw myself off and end the misery."

"You did?"

"Yep. Fortunately I came to my senses when I looked down at the bottom and thought of all those big boulders smashing me to a pulp. I also realized I'd be playing into her father's hands by showing I was too weak to confront life's problems head-on, proving I was unfit to be his daughter's husband."

"What did you do next?"

"I got on with my life. What else could I do?" Shakespeare answered. "I spent a lot of time trapping and hunting. Before long I heard that Blue Water's father had arranged her marriage to a warrior named Spotted Owl."

"Wait a minute," Nate interrupted. "Her father set the whole thing up? Didn't she have a say in it?"

"No," Shakespeare said. "It's a common practice in some tribes for the parents to arrange marriages. Sometimes the daughter doesn't even know the man she's going to wed."

"How can they do such a thing?" Nate wondered, appalled. It seemed to him that a woman should have a say in who she wanted to spend the rest of her life with, and he was glad his romance with Winona had developed naturally, based on the strong affections of both of them rather than the wishes of others.

"Easily," Shakespeare said. "You see, sometimes a father will set up a marriage to a warrior from a prominent family, one that has scores of horses and whose men are noted for their bravery. It's the father's way of moving up in the world, so to speak."

"At his daughter's expense," Nate stated in disapproval. He knew that many white women deliberately courted wealthy men so they would marry into money, and that white parents often pressured their daughters into rejecting the man the daughters loved and tying the knot with someone who had a fatter bank account. It was upsetting to learn that some Indians indulged in the same distasteful social practice.

"Well, what's done is done," Shakespeare said with an air of resignation. "Blue Water Woman married Spotted Owl and I saw nothing of her for two years or more. Then one day I met Buffalo Horn, who introduced me to his brother. Surprisingly, I found I liked Spotted Owl a lot. We became close friends."

"How did Blue Water Woman react?"

"She was friendly, nothing more. I figured any feelings she had for me were long gone. Then Spotted

Owl let me know that his older sister, Rainbow Woman, whose husband had died on a buffalo hunt, was quite fond of me." Shakespeare chuckled. "I'd seen her around and admired her appearance, but I never gave any thought to courting her until I learned she was interested in me."

"And you fell in love with her," Nate said, smiling.

"Love, love, nothing but love, still more!" Shakespeare quoted. "For, O, love's bow shoots buck and doe. The shaft confounds, not that it wounds, but tickles still the sore." He laughed. "Yes, I grew to love her more than I had ever loved anyone, including Blue Water Woman."

Trying to be philosophical, Nate commented, "All's well that ends well."

"Not quite, I'm afraid. Because a year and a half after I took Rainbow Woman as my wife, Blue Water Woman came up to me one day and confided that she still loved me with all her heart, that she liked Spotted Owl but he could never claim her devotion as I had."

"What did you say?" Nate inquired, intrigued by the tale. He couldn't imagine what it would be like to be loved by two women at the same time.

"I told her I was sorry to hear it because our relationship was over. I loved Rainbow Woman," Shakespeare related. "Blue Water Woman accepted the fact, but told me she would always care for me no matter what happened. Then she walked off."

"And now she's back in your life," Nate said.

"Which brings me to the reason I came to see you. Do you think I should marry her?"

Nate blinked in surprise. "That's a decision you must make on your own."

"At least give me your opinion," Shakespeare urged. "It's important to me." He reached up and scratched his beard. "I'm getting on in years, as you well know. I'm also sort of set in my ways. Taking Blue

Water Woman as my wife could be the biggest mistake I've ever made, and I've made some whoppers in my time."

Nate detected uncertainty in his friend's eyes, a sight he never thought he would see. "If you're asking my approval, I say go ahead. Unless, of course, you'd rather spend your last years alone, talking to yourself and spending your idle days dreaming about the grand old times."

Shakespeare thoughtfully nodded. "You don't hold back, do you?"

"You wanted to know."

"Thanks," Shakespeare said, and shoved upright. "You've hit the nail on the head. I'd much rather wake up in the morning lying beside a woman who cares for me, all warm and cozy, rather than wake up alone and cold and hugging my Hawken."

Nate laughed lightly.

"I'd better get a little sleep," Shakespeare said, yawning. "I want to be alert when Standing Bear makes his move."

"What do you think he'll do?"

"There's no telling. When a man has a powerful hankering for a woman, his body and mind stop working right. All he can think of is her. Standing Bear will do whatever he must to eliminate me as a rival." Shakespeare nodded and started to walk off. "I'll look you up after I'm rested."

"I'll be here," Nate said. He watched his friend depart, noticing the sun had partially risen. Standing, he moved off to find a spot where he could relieve himself. Two dozen yards downstream on Stinking Creek he found a stand of trees that adequately served his purpose. Once done, he strolled back to the lodge, enjoying the dawn; the happy chirping of the many birds, the growing warmth in the air, the sight of fish leaping in the creek. At times the wilderness resembled his ideal of Paradise on Earth, and he marveled that he had wasted so many years living among the brick and stone canyons of New York City, where the only wildlife he'd observed, other than birds, had been squirrels; the nearest thing to virgin forest had been overused parks.

He saw smoke curling upward from the lodge as he neared it. At the flap he paused and coughed loudly to let them know he was returning. He didn't want to barge in and accidentally catch Flower Woman changing clothes or doing something equally private. After several seconds he carefully parted the flap and peered within.

Flower Woman was breast feeding her baby. She smiled and continued, not the least bit concerned about exposing her breasts.

Wind In The Grass was seated by the fire, feeding small limbs to the flames. He glanced at the entrance, beamed, and signed, "You were up early. Did you sleep well?"

"Never slept better," Nate replied, entering. "I took a short walk." He went to his bedding and rolled up the blankets, then placed them to one side.

"Flower Woman will make breakfast as soon as Roaring Mountain is full," Wind In The Grass signed.

"There is no hurry," Nate responded.

"What would you like to do today?"

"Other than keeping an eye on Carcajou, I have nothing planned," Nate signed.

"We could go hunting," Wind In The Grass proposed.

Nate liked the idea. The family could use fresh game, and bagging a deer or an elk would be a fine way of repaying them for their hospitality. "I would like that," he noted.

They made small talk until Flower Woman finished

feeding the baby. She was just sorting through the parfleches for their food when everyone distinctly heard the sound of rushing feet and a second later a voice called out in the Flathead tongue. Nate tensed, recalling yesterday when the warrior brought news of Shakespeare's fight. He heard Wind In The Grass answer, and in popped a familiar face.

"Good morning, Grizzly Killer," Running Elk said. "I am sorry to bother you but something important has come up and we thought you would be interested."

Nate couldn't help but notice that Running Elk had completely ignored Wind In The Grass, a terrible breach of etiquette. "What is it?" he asked.

"Several of our men went out yesterday after buffalo. They found a war party of Blackfeet camped ten miles north of our village and came back to warn us. Buffalo Horn is leading some of our men against them. Would you like to come?"

"Is Shakespeare going along?"

"I asked, but he said he was too tired from being awake all night," Running Elk said.

Nate hesitated, reluctant to leave his mentor at the mercy of Standing Bear and the others.

"Twenty warriors are going," Running Elk went on. "Standing Bear, Bad Face, Wolf Ribs, and Smoke are among them."

"Oh?" Nate said, his interest piqued. Perhaps going would be a good idea. It would enable him to keep an eye on those four, and accomplish something else just as important. Without glancing at his host, he said, "What about Wind In The Grass? Has he been invited?"

Running Elk frowned and looked at the young warrior. "Buffalo Horn did not ask him."

"I'll go only if he does," Nate bluntly declared.

The statement made Running Elk's brow knit in deep thought. After a bit he sighed and nodded. "Very well. I am sure Buffalo Horn will agree. We will come get the two of you soon."

"We'll be ready," Nate promised.

Withdrawing from view, Running Elk ran off, his footsteps diminishing with the distance.

Wind In The Grass looked at Nate. "What was that all about?" he signed.

Nate explained, studying his host's face as he did. He saw hope flare in the warrior's eyes and knew he had made the right decision.

"Thank you," Wind In The Grass responded. "This is a chance for me to prove myself to the rest of the tribe."

"You will do fine," Nate assured him, while in the back of his mind he prayed that both of them would make it back in one piece. The Blackfeet were the scourge of the Rockies, the most warlike tribe in existence and justifiably noted for their fighting prowess. On top of all that, they positively loathed whites. If nothing else, he reflected wryly, the day was getting off to a rousing start.

Just so he lived to see the night.

Chapter Eleven

Nate had the stallion saddled and was standing outside the lodge talking to Wind In The Grass when the party of twenty warriors approached from the south, Buffalo Horn and Running Elk at the front. He glanced at the riders, tensing when he spied Standing Bear and the three other troublemakers riding near the middle of the group.

"Good morning, Grizzly Killer," Buffalo Horn greeted him with a friendly grin. "Are you ready to take Blackfeet scalps?"

"I'm ready to help you defend your territory," Nate amended, and swung into the saddle. It bothered him that Buffalo Horn didn't say a word to Wind In The Grass, who was now mounted beside him.

"We do not know how many Blackfeet there are, so we must be very careful," Buffalo Horn said.

"Why not be on the safe side and take more warriors along?" Nate proposed.

"And what if a large Blackfoot force attacks our

village while we are gone?" Buffalo Horn rejoined.
"No, the rest of our warriors must stay here to defend
our loved ones."

Nate nodded in understanding and hefted the
Hawken. "Well, I'm ready. Let's hit the trail."

"I would be honored if you would ride at my side,"
Buffalo Horn said, and motioned to his left.

"My friend and I will be glad to," Nate said,
indicating Wind In The Grass with a jerk of his
thumb.

Buffalo Horn glanced at the young warrior, disapproval plainly etched in his face. "As you wish," he
said coldly, with the same enthusiasm as a man who
had been asked to keep company with a carrier of the
plague. He jabbed his horse with his heels, moving
out.

Nate turned the stallion, falling in with the group,
glancing over his shoulder at Standing Bear and Bad
Face, both of whom glared. He didn't like having his
back to them, but he doubted they would do anything
when there were so many others around. They certainly wouldn't shoot him in the back; such a cowardly act
would get them expelled from the tribe.

Buffalo Horn led them to Stinking Creek, crossed it
at a shallow point, and continued northward into a
narrow valley that wound among foothills.

As always, Nate reveled in the abundant wildlife.
He spotted a herd of deer, four elk, and a large hawk
circling high overhead, all within the first mile. Looking to his left, he found Wind In The Grass riding
proudly, head held high, and he hoped he hadn't made
a mistake by having the young warrior brought along.
If Wind In The Grass should be killed, he'd never
forgive himself for sticking his big nose in and trying
to set things straight.

At the end of the valley they passed through a gap
between two hills, crossed a meadow, and skirted a

snow crowned mountain by traveling along its base to the west.

"We are about half the distance to the Blackfoot camp," Buffalo Horn said to Nate. "Our hunters saw their fort near Still Lake."

Nate had seen such "forts" before. Of all the tribes with which he was familiar, only the Blackfeet used them, perhaps because they preferred to conduct their raids on foot instead of on horseback, and were therefore more vulnerable to attack. When a Blackfoot war party was in enemy country and made camp at night, or when they were set upon by those they intended to raid, the Blackfeet constructed large conical forts of stout limbs, or brush forts if there wasn't the time, and defended themselves with habitual vigor.

"I doubt they are still there," Buffalo Horn remarked. "They were probably staying near the lake for the night. We might run into them somewhere along the way."

"Do you think they know where your village is?" Nate asked.

"If not, you can be sure they are looking for it very hard. At least once every three or four moons they raid us, stealing some of our horses and killing a few of our warriors. This time we will give them a surprise."

"Have you ever raided them?"

"Two summers ago we did."

"That's the only time in recent years?"

Buffalo Horn's features seemed to cloud over. "Their territory is far to the northeast. They have many, many villages, and their warriors are everywhere. Few tribes ever send raiding parties into the country of the Blackfeet because most never come back."

Nate thoughtfully pursed his lips. Quite obviously the Flatheads, like the majority of other tribes, lived in fear of the Blackfeet. Buffalo Horn would never admit as much, but Nate suspected that was the real reason the Flatheads had rarely given the Blackfeet a taste of their own medicine.

They went around another mountain and slanted up the gradually tapering slope of the next one, following a well-worn game trail. The narrow track of dirt and flattened grass forced them to ride in single file.

Nate stayed alert, scanning the forest below and the landscape in all directions. There was nothing to indicate the Blackfeet were anywhere around. They climbed several hundred feet, then halted when Buffalo Horn reigned up. "Is something wrong?" Nate inquired.

The Flathead pointed northward. "We are close now. I hoped we would see the smoke from their fire."

Only clear, azure sky dominated the horizon beyond.

Winding down the trail, they entered dense forest consisting of various kinds of pine trees. Squirrels scampered from limb to limb and startled rabbits bounded off into the brush. After traveling over a mile, Buffalo Horn halted once more. "From here we should walk," he declared, and went to swing down.

"Why not let Wind In The Grass watch our horses?" Nate suggested.

Buffalo Horn paused. "Why him?"

"Why not?"

"I would like another warrior to watch them."

"Wind In The Grass will do just fine."

"Do not ask me to do this," Buffalo Horn said, scowling.

"I must. Please. For me," Nate asked.

The Flathead glanced at the young warrior, then at Running Elk. "What do you say?"

"Grizzly Killer is Carcajou's close friend," Running Elk replied.

Perturbed but trying hard not to show it, Buffalo Horn gave a curt nod and dismounted. "Very well. Wind In The Grass will tend our animals."

"Thank you," Nate said, sliding to the ground. He heard Running Elk translate for the benefit of Wind In The Grass, who then beamed and gazed gratefully at him. He smiled, winked, and joined the flow of warriors who were following Buffalo Horn deeper into the forest. As luck would have it, he was only a yard in front of Standing Bear, who was carrying a bow. An odd itch developed between his shoulder blades as he walked ahead of the embittered warrior, and he was glad when they came to a clearing and stopped so he could pass other Flatheads and catch up with Buffalo Horn and Running Elk.

The Flatheads set about preparing themselves; nocking bows, drawing knives, hefting war clubs and lances, and, in the case of the few with firearms, verifying their weapons were loaded.

Buffalo Horn double-checked his rifle, then motioned for them to proceed. The warriors spread out, taking advantage of all available cover, moving from tree to tree and bush to bush. For over a hundred yards they continued in this fashion, and then the forest began to thin out.

Nate spied a body of water ahead and surmised it to be Still Lake. He scanned the shoreline but saw no sign of the Blackfoot forts, no sign of anything moving. Perhaps, he reflected, the Blackfeet had long since departed in another direction. As he neared the water, he moved slower, his thumb curled around the Hawken's hammer.

The deep blue surface of the lake resembled polished glass. Unruffled by even the tiniest wave, it gave the illusion of being solid rather than liquid. There was no evidence of fish, and a complete lack of waterfowl.

The observation struck Nate as strange. Every mountain lake he knew of teemed with life. Why not this one? He wondered if there might be a substance in the water that the animals didn't like.

Glancing to his left, he finally spotted the conical forts. There were three of them aligned in a row on the west shore, at the edge of the trees so they would blend in from a distance. Not a soul was around. He angled toward them, Buffalo Horn and Running Elk a few yards ahead.

Several warriors who were off on the left increased their pace and warily approached the makeshift structures. They were studies in nervous energy, gazing every which way, treading lightly and ready to bolt at the first hint of hostility.

Buffalo Horn and Running Elk stopped. So did the rest.

Nate followed their example. He figured they had more experience in Indian warfare than he did, and relied on their discretion. Apprehensively, he watched four braves move from concealment and dash to the forts. The warriors quickly searched each one, then emerged, relieved and all smiles, and beckoned for their fellows to join them. Almost as one, the Flatheads rose and walked forward.

Reluctantly, Nate stood. He scoured the woods behind the forts and saw nothing move, but he felt uneasy about waltzing into the open without having conducted a thorough check of the woodland around Still Lake. Consequently, he trailed behind the rest of the Flatheads, deliberately dawdling.

The warriors conversed loudly, discussing the situation, Buffalo Horn doing most of the talking.

Nate halted after walking only fifteen feet. His mind was shrieking a warning that things were not as they seemed, that they should all get out of there before something terrible happened. But he was loathe to say anything for fear of coming across as a fool if there was no danger.

What should he do?

Then he remembered advice once dispensed by Shakespeare: "Always rely on your gut feelings, your intuition. The Great Mystery gave it to you for a reason. If more folks used theirs on a regular basis, they would be a lot better off."

The Flatheads were inspecting the forts. A few were searching the ground for tracks.

"Buffalo Horn," Nate called out, finally making up his mind.

Both Buffalo Horn and Running Elk turned. "What is it, Grizzly Killer?" the former asked.

"Get the warriors away from there," Nate said urgently.

"Why? What is wrong?"

"I'm not sure," Nate admitted, his eyes roving over the wall of vegetation to the rear of the forts. Suddenly he saw a flicker of motion, then another, motions that resolved themselves into the shadowy figures of stalking Blackfeet. The sight sent a chill rippling down his spine, but he still retained the presence of mind to cry out, "Behind you! It's a trap!"

The Flatheads, startled by the cry, gazed about in confusion. Since most didn't speak English, they had no idea why he had yelled although they fully appreciated the manifest distress in his agitated tone.

All except Buffalo Horn and Running Elk, who both spun in alarm. They saw the danger, but they were too late to prevent the inevitable.

A swarm of arrows streaked out of the vegetation

attended by the blasting of a number of fusees. In the blink of an eye six of the Flatheads were down, dead, and three others were staggering, pierced by shafts or wounded by balls.

Buffalo Horn bellowed and the Flatheads retreated, helping those who were wounded. Harsh whoops erupted in the foliage and another swarm of whizzing arrows cleaved the air. It was a slaughter. Five more Flatheads were slain, two more wounded. Now there were only four untouched Flatheads left; Buffalo Horn, Running Elk, Standing Bear, and Bad Face.

Nate saw a Blackfoot armed with a fusee materialize and point the weapon at the fleeing Flatheads. Snapping the Hawken to his right shoulder, he fired before the Blackfoot could. The warrior fell, the fusee falling from his hands. Back-pedaling, Nate reloaded on the run, reaching the trees well ahead of the Flatheads. He had to provide covering fire or they were all dead.

His fingers flew faster than they ever had before. First he had to pour in the proper amount of powder, then place a patch around the ball and insert it, then use the ramrod to press the ball down to the bottom of the barrel. All the while the Blackfeet were loosing arrows. One of the wounded Flatheads toppled, a shaft jutting from the center of his chest.

Nate spied another Blackfoot at the opposite tree line and took hasty aim. The man was bringing a bow vertical, about to let fly. Not this time, Nate thought, and let the Hawken punctuate his intent.

The ball took the Blackfoot in the head, catapulting him backwards.

Now Buffalo Horn and the other survivors reached the temporary shelter of the woods near Nate. They pressed onward, aware their lives hung in the balance if they failed to reach their mounts.

Nate brought up the rear, reloading yet again. He could see Blackfeet emerging from behind the forts. Eight. Ten. Twelve. They screeched, hefted their various weapons, and raced in pursuit.

The situation was desperate. Nate could scarcely believe that in the span of less than a minute the Flathead force had been decimated. He hoped Wind In The Grass had heard the gunfire and would bring their horses at a gallop. Then, out of the corner of his eye, he spotted running forms, and looking in that direction he beheld a sight that compounded their desperation.

Running along the south shore, apparently planning to reinforce their companions, were more Blackfeet.

Chapter Twelve

Nate pointed at the reinforcements and shouted to Buffalo Horn, "Here come more!"

The Flathead looked, his features betraying his anxiety. He was supporting another warrior wounded in the thigh. Firming his grip, he picked up the pace.

Running Elk shot an arrow that dropped the foremost Blackfoot to their rear.

Another enemy, who was trying to swing to the west to outflank the Flatheads, attracted Nate's attention. He aimed as best he could while on the run and fired, uncertain whether he would score a hit. The Blackfoot pitched forward and was still.

Not bad shooting, Nate complimented himself, reloading. But it hardly slowed the Blackfeet, who were flitting from tree trunk to tree trunk with the agility of antelope. He wished he knew which one was their leader. Shakespeare had mentioned that when battling a war party, always go for the chief or the warrior in charge. When the top man fell, frequently the rest would take the body and fall back to regroup, or they would discontinue the fight if they felt the death of their leader was a bad omen.

Although the Blackfeet were still sending arrows and a few fusee balls after the fleeing Flatheads, most of their shots missed, deflected by the intervening brush or fired in such haste the aim was off.

Nate fared better. Twice he downed Blackfeet, and the deadly retort of his rifle was serving to keep the group to the rear at bay. Those to the south were not yet close enough to justify diverting his attention from the more immediate menace of those dogging the Flatheads' heels.

The running battle continued for another hundred yards. Evidently knowing they had the upper hand and would soon bring the Flatheads at bay, the Blackfeet made no effort to mount a concerted rush, even after the second group of six warriors joined the first.

Reloading feverishly time and again, Nate did his utmost to buy the Flatheads more time. He glanced over his shoulder repeatedly, expecting to see Wind In The Grass bringing the horses, but his friend had yet to show.

The Flatheads came to a knoll and skirted its base on the right. They were beginning to tire, and one of the wounded men was ready to keel over at any second. A ten-foot high boulder in their path became their sanctuary as they all took shelter in its comforting shadow.

Nate halted beside the boulder, his rifle leveled, seeking another target. The crafty Blackfeet had learned their lesson; his marksmanship was forcing them to stay well back and well hidden.

Buffalo Horn deposited the wounded warrior he had been assisting on the ground and turned to Nate. "Go for the horses. We will wait here."

Surprised at the request and disinclined to desert them, Nate shook his head. "I'm not leaving you."

"Our only hope is the horses," Buffalo Horn stressed, gripping Nate's arm. "We can hold them off until you return."

"If the horses are still there," Running Elk interjected bitterly.

Nate opened his mouth to object again when an arrow flashed out of nowhere, missing his face by less than an inch and almost striking Buffalo Horn in the abdomen. The tall Flathead looked into his eyes, pleading silently. He realized he had no choice. Either he retrieved the mounts, or they would be massacred to the last man. "All right," he said, alertly scanning the woods while moving backwards. "I'll go get them."

"Hurry," Buffalo Horn urged.

Whirling, Nate took only four strides when he heard a sound that was more wonderful than any music ever played; the thundering drum of many horses, coming directly toward him. He spotted them the next instant.

Wind In The Grass was riding at a reckless pace, using only his legs to guide his animal, his hands full with the long reins of the animals he was leading, his muscles straining in rippling relief as he pulled them in his wake.

"There!" Nate shouted, elated, and turned to help a wounded Flathead make for their salvation.

The Blackfeet perceived their quarry might escape and intensified their attack, raining down arrows in a steady hail of lethal barbed points. Venting their war whoops, many broke from cover to try and overtake the Flatheads.

Nate saw Wind In The Grass struggling valiantly to keep the horses under control. With ten trailing from either arm, the mounts were bunched together and demonstrating their resentment of the claustrophobic treatment by jerking their heads back and causing no end of trouble.

Wind In The Grass stopped fifteen feet away. He leaned forward, breathing heavily from his strenuous exertion, sweat beading his forehead.

An impetuous Blackfoot, screaming crazily, sprinted straight at the Flatheads.

Pivoting, Nate let go of the wounded warrior, sighted, and squeezed off a shot that hit the Blackfoot between the eyes. The warrior did a complete revolution on one heel, then collapsed as if his legs were made of potter's clay. Without bothering to reload, Nate dashed to the horses.

The wounded Flatheads were being hurriedly assisted onto horses. An arrow smacked into a riderless horse, causing it to neigh in terror and rear back on its hind legs, throwing several other horses into a panic.

Nate swung onto his stallion. He rode a few yards toward the converging Blackfeet, drew a flintlock, and fired the big pistol into the chest of the closest adversary. The man died soundlessly, prompting the rest to scatter, seeking protective cover. In a smooth motion Nate wedged the pistol under his belt and drew the second flintlock. He risked a look back. The eight surviving Flatheads, four of whom were wounded, were now mounted beside Wind In The Grass.

Buffalo Horn motioned and they goaded their animals into a gallop, heading southward. He stayed, waving his arms and shouting to get the riderless animals to scatter.

Comprehending, Nate wheeled the stallion and helped drive the horses off to prevent the Blackfeet from catching them. No sooner had the last horse galloped off than he did the same alongside Buffalo Horn, trailing the ragtag remains of the once proud band of noble avengers.

A few last arrows, parting shots from the infuriated Blackfeet, fell close behind the departing Flatheads, but none of the shafts came close enough to claim additional lives.

Sweet relief coursed through Nate as their escape became apparent. He thought of all the Flatheads who had died because of blatant carelessness and wished he had shouted a warning just a few seconds sooner. Perhaps more would have lived. Then again, he knew he shouldn't blame himself for their own neglect. He'd done all he could to help them when they'd needed help the most.

Buffalo Horn took the lead, riding hard for almost a mile. He abruptly reined up in a clearing and turned, issuing directions to the warriors. In short order the four wounded men were placed on the grass where the gravity of their individual conditions could be adequately gauged.

Nate stayed on his stallion, turned sideways in the saddle so he could watch their back trail. Thankfully, the Blackfeet had been left far behind. Fleet as they were, they were no match for horses. He glanced at Buffalo Horn, who was examining the last injured warrior. "How are they?"

"Not good, I am afraid. Three of them will never make it to our village."

"What will you do?"

"Tend to them the best we can and keep going. It is too dangerous to stay here very long with the Blackfeet on the prowl."

"I'll keep watch," Nate offered, and did just that while reloading his guns.

Running Elk and Standing Bear went into the woods and returned carrying several leaves and a poultice they had prepared from strictly herbal substances. The mixture was applied to the wounds of each warrior, and after allowing the men to rest for a bit, Buffalo Horn gave instructions and mounted again.

Nate brought up the rear as they moved out, constantly scanning the forest, and not until two more miles were behind them was he convinced they had truly escaped. At that point, as they crossed over a low knoll, one of the wounded warriors cried out plaintively and pitched from his animal. The body was draped over the horse and on they went.

He could well imagine the reception they would receive at the village since he'd witnessed such pitiable scenes of mass mourning before among the Shoshones. And he did not envy Buffalo Horn one bit. Warriors who took it upon themselves to lead war parties were held strictly accountable if that war party met disaster, and the debacle at Still Lake might well effect Buffalo Horn's social standing and warrior status in the tribe.

Suddenly he realized Standing Bear was looking at him and wondered why. It was regrettable, he mused, that Shakespeare's rival and Bad Face had both survived the battle. Had they perished, his friend's problem would be solved and there would be nothing to prevent him from returning to Winona.

Nate thought of her often on the return trip, of the loneliness she must be experiencing because of his loyalty to Shakespeare. But he couldn't leave yet, not until Standing Bear and Bad Face were taken care of.

By midafternoon two more of the wounded Flatheads died. Buffalo Horn and the rest barely spoke the entire time. An oppressive atmosphere hovered around them, a pall of death they were unable to shake.

When Nate finally spotted the village, he smiled

happily. Once again a shout went up and Flatheads converged from all directions. Instead of smiling and laughing, though, they were grim and silent. Where twenty-two men had gone off to slay Blackfeet, only seven were coming back, a staggering toll the warrior ranks could ill afford since the women already outnumbered the men by a considerable margin.

He glanced at Wind In The Grass, who had also been unusually quiet, and noted profound sadness in the young warrior's eyes. Both times that Wind In The Grass had gone on raids, the raiding parties had met disaster. Knowing how superstitious the Indians were, he speculated on whether the tribe might decide Wind In The Grass was somehow jinxed, a living bad omen.

Wails arose from a number of women as the party drew nearer and the wives could see who was there and who was missing. The lamentations became more general as Buffalo Horn led the weary warriors in among the lodges. One of the women rushed up to the horse bearing the wounded man and clutched at his leg, sobbing softly. Friends came to help her, and together they took the wounded man off toward his own teepee.

Buffalo Horn turned and gazed at Nate and Wind In The Grass. "I thank both of you for going along. All of us might have been killed if not for the two of you," he said in English, then repeated the words in his own tongue.

Wind In The Grass mustered a wan smile at the news, replied briefly, and wheeled his horse toward Stinking Creek.

About to tag along, Nate paused. His host might like to be alone with Flower Woman for a while. He'd go there later. For now, he faced Buffalo Horn. "I understand Shakespeare is staying with you."

"Yes. Come. We will go there," Buffalo Horn said, heading eastward.

The warrior's dejected expression tugged at Nate's sympathy. "Try to cheer up," he advised. "One day you'll get your revenge on the Blackfeet."

"If I go on a raid again, perhaps."

"You may not?"

"No. My medicine failed me. White men might call it bad luck, but my people know better. My spirit guide did not watch over me this time as in the past and I must find out why."

Nate shrugged. "I think you're being too hard on yourself. It could have happened to anyone."

"You are trying to be kind," Buffalo Horn said. "If you knew our ways better, you would understand how serious this is. It all goes back to when I was sixteen and I went into the mountains by myself on a vision quest. I fasted for seven days and seven nights, and then the vision came to me."

"What kind of vision?" Nate inquired when the warrior stopped, burning with curiosity.

Buffalo Horn's face lit up at the memory. "It was wonderful. A spirit being, a great fiery buffalo with only one bright red horn, appeared to me and offered to be my personal guardian. It taught me a prayer I must say every day and a ritual I must do once a month to keep my charm filled with power."

"Your charm?"

Nodding, Buffalo Horn reached into a pouch hanging on his left hip and extracted the smooth, severed tip of a buffalo horn. "This is my special charm. Without it, I will surely die."

"I see," Nate said, struggling inwardly with acceptance of the notion. Although he keenly admired most aspects of Indian life, he found their extreme fascination with certain superstitions rather bothersome. He had to remind himself that he had never gone on a vision quest, and had no cause to think lightly of a practice most tribes had indulged in for more years than anyone could recollect. "What will you do?" he asked.

"I will try to contact my spirit guide and find out why my charm has lost its power."

"How do you go about doing that?"

"I will go off and not eat until the fiery buffalo appears to me."

"What if it doesn't?"

"Then I die."

Chapter Thirteen

Shakespeare was seated outside of Buffalo Horn's lodge cleaning his rifle when Nate and Buffalo Horn arrived. He took one look and stood, coming out to meet them. "How did it go?" he inquired.

Nate shook his head.

"The Blackfeet were waiting for us," Buffalo Horn said sadly. "We were ambushed and most of our warriors were killed. By now the Blackfeet have taken their scalps and cut their bodies into pieces."

"I'm sorry," Shakespeare said sincerely.

Buffalo Horn halted and dropped to the grass. A heavyset woman emerged from the teepee, hurrying toward him. They spoke in the Flathead language for a bit, then both went inside.

"He's taking it hard," Nate commented, dismounting.

"He has reason to," Shakespeare said, and placed a hand on the younger man's shoulder. "I'm glad nothing happened to you. I wouldn't want to bear the bad tidings to Winona."

"Is that the only reason?"

Shakespeare grinned. "The only one I can think of at the moment." He motioned at the ground. "Sit down and tell me everything that happened."

Keeping to the essential facts, Nate related the day's events, concluding with a mention of Buffalo Horn's intention to try and contact the spirit guide.

"At his age?" Shakespeare said. "Any extended time without food and water could kill him."

"So he said."

"At my age, I'm not too partial to losing old friends. There aren't all that many left in this world."

"Think you can talk him out of it?"

Shakespeare stared at the lodge entrance, his mouth curling downward. "Not very likely. To an Indian, a guardian spirit is as much a part of his life as is breathing and eating. No warrior can be without one. Buffalo Horn will do anything to restore the power to his charm now that he believes it's not effective."

"So there's nothing you can do?" Nate asked.

"Pray for the best."

Nate leaned back on his palms. "Since you have a moment, there's something else I'd like to bring up."

"What?"

"Standing Bear. Now that Smoke and Wolf Ribs are dead, do you figure he'll back down and leave you alone?"

The mountain man chuckled. "Does a grizzly ever run from a scrap of meat? No. And just because two of Standing Bear's best friends are dead won't mean a thing to him. He'll still try to kill me. I just don't know when or how."

"And what about the lady you're fighting over? Have you given her your decision yet?"

"Not yet. I see her this evening. She's living in the same lodge she shared with Spotted Owl, not far from where Wind In The Grass has his teepee."

"Which reminds me," Nate said, rising. "I should go see how he's doing. He didn't seem too happy about the outcome of the raid."

"At least he redeemed himself with the horses," Shakespeare noted, also standing. "The next time a war party goes out, hopefully they won't hesitate to take him along."

Stepping to the stallion, Nate swung up. "Take care of yourself."

A peculiar expression lined Shakespeare's face. "The single and peculiar life is bound with all the strength and armour of the mind to keep itself from noyance. But much more that spirit upon whose weal depends and rest the lives of many," he quoted.

"What?"

"Arm you, I pray you, to this speedy voyage, for we will fetters put about this fear, which now goes too free-footed."

"Be honest with me, Shakespeare," Nate said, smiling. "Do you have any idea what you just said?"

"Certainly," McNair replied indignantly. "I advised you to take good care of yourself."

"You could have fooled me," Nate said, and headed toward the north end of the village. Everywhere there were sad faces, warriors and women walking around in abject depression because of the outcome of the raid. Even the children were subdued now, either with their parents inside their lodges or sitting around outside and conversing in hushed tones. He felt strangely out of place, as if he was witnessing very private grief not meant for outsiders to observe.

When he was only forty yards or so from his destination, he reined up in surprise. Directly ahead, standing in front of a lodge, were Blue Water Woman and Bad Face. They appeared to be arguing, although both were keeping their voices down. Bad Face gestured angrily over and over.

What do I do? Nate asked himself. He didn't want to meddle, but he didn't want to sit there and do nothing while Bad Face berated his mentor's future wife. Compromising, he slanted the Hawken across his thighs and rode boldly up to them, a friendly grin plastered on his lips. "Howdy, Blue Water Woman," he said.

They both glanced up. Bad Face instantly glowered while Blue Water Woman seemed relieved.

"Hello, Grizzly Killer," she greeted him. "I have heard you fought very bravely today."

Nate fixed his eyes on the warrior. "Did Bad Face tell you that? I didn't know he was so considerate. Thank him for me."

Blue Water Woman laughed. "It was someone else who told me. Bad Face does not hold a very high opinion of you."

"I would never have known," Nate said, and bluntly came to the point. "Is he bothering you?"

"He wants me to accompany him to go see Standing Bear, but I have refused."

The burly warrior had taken all the English he was about to. His hands flew in sharp motions as he signed, "Leave us in peace, Grizzly Killer. This does not concern you."

Instead of signing a response, Nate simply shifted so the barrel of the Hawken was trained on Bad Face's chest. He made no move to lift the weapon or overtly threaten the Flathead in any way, but Bad Face understood his meaning. For a moment they locked eyes in a silent battle of wills as each measured up the other.

Bad Face finally spun and stalked off.

"Thank you, Grizzly Killer," Blue Water Woman said. "Standing Bear is becoming more persistent than I thought he would."

"Why did he send Bad Face instead of coming in person?"

"Because Standing Bear is a very proud man and he could never bring himself to beg me to pay his teepee a visit. So he sent Bad Face in his place."

"You'd better stay on your guard," Nate suggested. "I wouldn't put anything past those two."

"They would never harm me. Such an act would get them expelled from the tribe for the rest of their lives."

"In any case, if you need me I'm staying with Wind In The Grass," Nate mentioned, pointing at the appropriate lodge. "Just give a holler and I'll come running."

"You are quite kind. I can see why Carcajou respects you so highly. He thinks of you as the son he never had."

"He does?" Nate said, flattered by the compliment. "He's never told me that."

"Men are not as open with secrets of the heart as are women. I believe the Great Mystery made them inferior in that respect."

"Sounds like something my wife would say," Nate remarked.

Blue Water Woman nodded. "Women are wiser in such matters than men. All men think about is hunting and fighting and making love."

Shocked by her frank assertion, Nate could only mumble, "Well, not all men."

"Most," Blue Water Woman said. "There are a few who look deeper into themselves and discover the true meaning of life, men like Carcajou."

Nate leaned forward, his curiosity aroused. "What is the true meaning of life?"

"You will find it one day."

"That's not much of an answer."

"It is the only answer."

Puzzled, Nate straightened. He was beginning to understand the reason Shakespeare cared for her so much. They were a perfect match; they both spoke in circles. "If you say so," he said, tightening his grip on the reins.

"Time, Grizzly Killer, uncovers all."

"Oh," Nate said, and coughed lightly. "Well, it's about time I went to see Wind In The Grass. Nice talking to you again."

"The same here. Come visit me soon," Blue Water Woman requested, reaching up to run her right hand along her long hair, smoothing it over her shoulder.

"I will," Nate promised, and rode toward his host's lodge, his growling stomach reminding him that he could use some food. He wondered if Flower Woman had more tasty buffalo stew, his mouth watering at the thought.

As Nate drew up in front of the lodge he noticed the flap was tied up. According to Indian etiquette, that meant any friend of the owner could enter without having to announce himself. Consequently, he dismounted, ground-hitched the stallion, and went in with a smile on his face.

Seated at the customary spot, his head held high, was Wind In The Grass. Cradled in his lap was his son. Flower Woman was busily preparing a meal over the crackling fire. She shifted as Nate entered and beamed, her hands moving fluidly. "I am the happiest woman alive this day. My husband has proven himself to the tribe. Now no one will speak badly of him."

"I know," Nate signed in return, and waited for his host to indicate where he should sit, which turned out to be the seat of honor. He walked over and sank down with a sigh.

"Since this is a special day, I am using the last of our

meat to make a special meal," Flower Woman signed.
"I hope you will like it."

"I will," Nate assured her, and looked at Wind In
The Grass. Despite the joyous occasion, the young
warrior's countenance was tinged with melancholy.
"Is something wrong?" he inquired.

"I am sad for the lives of all the brave men who died
today," Wind In The Grass responded. "Had I
brought the horses sooner, some more might have
lived."

"I am sure you did the best you could."

Wind In The Grass was still for a moment. "I tried
to come at the sound of the first shots, but several of
the horses gave me trouble. It took all of my strength
to bring them."

"I saw you," Nate reminded him. "We all did. You
were doing all any man could do. No one will blame
you for anything." He lowered his hands for a second.
"You should know that Buffalo Horn is taking all of
the blame for the deaths on his shoulders. He says it is
because his charm has lost its power."

Flower Woman uttered a loud snort. "I told you,"
she admonished her husband. "I said that you were
being too hard on yourself. Now the whole tribe will
know Buffalo Horn is to blame."

"I think they are all to blame," Nate signed.

Both Flatheads fixed perplexed expressions on him.
"Why?" Wind In The Grass asked.

In detail, Nate signed the story of the blunder the
Flatheads had committed by walking right up to the
Blackfoot forts, exposing themselves to the hidden
ambushers. He explained that they should have
checked the surrounding area before venturing into
the open, and told how his own feeling had saved his
life.

"It is true what they say," Wind In The Grass said

when the tale was done. "The Great Mystery is strong in you."

"Who says?" Nate asked.

"Everyone."

Nate wondered just how much talking the Flatheads had been doing behind his back about the exaggerated accounts of his exploits or of his battle with Mad Dog. Sometimes it seemed as if most people had nothing better to do than sit around and gossip like a quilting circle of elderly matrons.

Flower Woman took a step toward him. "How many Blackfeet did you kill, Grizzly Killer?"

"I did not count them," Nate said.

"Was it many?" she persisted.

"No. Six or seven, I believe."

The statement caused Flower Woman to step back again, but this time in astonishment. She gazed at her husband and signed, "Now I understand. Truly this is the highest honor we have ever had."

"What is she talking about?" Nate inquired, looking at his host.

"You have done more for me in the eyes of my people by staying with me than I did today by bringing the horses," Wind In The Grass said, and placed a hand on Nate's shoulder in friendly gratitude. "Among our tribe, a man is not worth anything if he is not brave. And the braver he is, the more enemies he slays in battle, the more courage he demonstrates, and the more honored he becomes. Other warriors always want to have such brave men as guests at their meals, or to have these brave ones visit often."

Nate understood. By associating with a highly regarded warrior, another man could enhance his own social prestige. In certain ways, he reflected, Indian culture was much like white culture, only in the white culture it was those with the most money who were so highly esteemed. Come to think of it, he decided, the Indian way was infinitely better.

"You wait and see," Wind In The Grass signed. "Having you here will make my lodge very popular."

As if in confirmation, a shadow darkened the entrance a heartbeat before a warrior entered, none other than White Eagle, the chief of the village.

Chapter Fourteen

Wind In The Grass, clearly startled, leaped to his feet and warmly greeted the aged warrior in their mutual tongue. Stepping forward, he motioned for White Eagle to take a seat.

Nate had noticed Flower Woman stiffen at the chief's entrance, leading him to deduce this was a singular event. It might well be the very first time White Eagle had paid them a visit. He nodded at the chief and made the sign for a friendly greeting.

White Eagle returned the courtesy as he sat down, then went on in extended sign language while looking at Wind In The Grass. "I am honored to be in the lodge of a man who did so well today. Buffalo Horn has told me that you carefully watched the horses and brought them as soon as you could after the Blackfeet ambushed our war party."

Pride brightened the young warrior's eyes as he replied, "I only did what was expected of me."

"You did well," White Eagle said, then paused to glance at Nate before continuing. "If you do not mind,

Wind In The Grass, we will use sign language to discuss the matter I have come to talk about, out of respect to your other guest."

"Had you not asked, I would have requested that we do so," Wind In The Grass responded. "I would not want to be impolite to Grizzly Killer."

White Eagle nodded. "Very well." He focused on Nate. "Grizzly Killer, if you would be so kind, I would like to hear your version of the events at Still Lake today."

"I would be happy to tell you," Nate replied, although in the back of his mind he wondered why the chief was specifically asking him when any of the surviving warriors could also provide a factual account. Dutifully, he launched into an extended recital of the fiasco, being careful not to attribute blame to anyone, and emphasizing at the end the outstanding job done by Wind In The Grass. Out of the corner of his eye he saw Flower Woman swell with affection for her spouse.

White Eagle bowed his head when Nate finished, his forehead furrowed in deep concentration. Finally he looked up and frowned. "Then it is worse than I thought," he signed.

"What is?" Wind In The Grass inquired.

"Those Blackfeet defeated our band soundly. I suspect they were able to catch some of our scattered horses and are now using them as their own. There is a chance they will mount another attack."

Nate raised his hands. "Surely the Blackfeet are on their way back to their own country now with the horses and the scalps they collected. Why would they stay in the area?"

"To get *more* horses and scalps," White Eagle said. "Blackfeet do not give up easily. I have known them to raid a village one day, then come back the very next day and raid it again."

Clever tactic, Nate reflected, since no one in the village would expect another attack so soon after the first incident.

"And even if they are not planning a raid on the village, they might be hiding out there waiting to ambush one of our hunting parties or hoping to steal some of our women when they go out foraging for food and herbs."

"Post more sentries," Nate proposed. "And do not let any women leave the village unless they are accompanied by warriors."

"Sound suggestions," White Eagle said, "ones I have already put into effect."

"Then all you can do is hope for the best," Nate signed.

"That, and one more thing."

"What?"

White Eagle gave each of them a meaningful stare. "I was thinking of sending out two or three men to see if the Blackfeet have departed our territory."

It took all of Nate's self-control to keep from frowning and thus insulting the chief. He knew who White Eagle had in mind, and it bothered him. Why couldn't they send out several of their own warriors? Why rely on him? The answer, ironically enough, was obvious; he was the great Grizzly Killer.

"I have already asked Carcajou and he has said he will go," White Eagle disclosed. "Would the two of you like to go along with him?"

"Wherever Carcajou goes, I go," Nate signed.

"And I would be glad to accompany them," Wind In The Grass answered.

"Good," White Eagle said. "It would be best if you waited until the rising of the sun. You will need plenty of rest after all you have been through today."

"We will be ready," Nate signed, then cocked his head when he heard the drumming of hooves from outside. Moments later the animal halted close to the entrance, footsteps sounded, and in came its rider. He smiled at the familiar figure and said in English, "Hello, Shakespeare."

The mountain man grinned and nodded. "Has White Eagle told you what he has in mind?"

"Yes."

"Figured as much. That's why I rode right over," Shakespeare said, then switched to sign language. "Greetings, Wind In The Grass and Flower Woman. I am honored to be in your lodge." He glanced at the chief. "And greetings again to you, White Eagle."

"Please, sit down," Wind In The Grass signed.

"Another time, perhaps," Shakespeare signed. "I can not stay long." He squatted beside the cooking fire. "I knew White Eagle was coming here to ask you to go with me to check on the Blackfeet. Have you both agreed?"

"Of course," Wind In The Grass replied.

Nate let a bob of his chin be his answer.

"I figured you would," Shakespeare said, "which is why I wanted to let you know right away that we will be leaving after dark."

Wind In The Grass appeared uneasy at the news. "Tonight?" he asked.

"Yes," Shakespeare said, and lifted his right arm to point at an angle toward the east, approximately twelve inches above an imaginary horizon. "When the moon is that high."

Nate could tell from the expressions on the Flatheads that none of them were very fond of the idea, and he knew the reason. Many Indians, as Shakespeare had taught him, rarely traveled at night; most of those in the Rockies and those dwelling on the plains farther east ventured abroad only between dawn and sunset. There were notable exceptions to the general rule, such as war parties who occasionally took advantage of the night to take enemies by surprise, and the dreaded Apaches who lived far to the southwest and reportedly preferred traveling after the sun went down rather than during the day.

"I will be ready," Wind In The Grass signed.

"Why not wait until morning?" White Eagle asked. "Riding at night is very dangerous. A man can not see as well, and the grizzlies, the long tailed cats, and the wolves are everywhere."

"We have a better chance of spotting the Blackfeet from a distance after dark," Shakespeare noted, and vented a reassuring chuckle. "I know what I'm doing. Trust me."

"I would never doubt you, Carcajou," White Eagle said. "I know you have the welfare of our people at heart."

"Thank you," Shakespeare said, standing and gazing at Nate and Wind In The Grass. "I just wanted to let you know ahead of time so the two of you can get some sleep before we leave."

"Appreciate it," Nate said.

"I will see both of you later," Shakespeare signed, and departed hastily.

Nate figured his friend was going to see Blue Water Woman, and he realized he should tell Shakespeare about the argument with Bad Face. But as he put his hands down to push to his feet, he heard Shakespeare's mount hurry off. Shrugging, he relaxed, certain Blue Water Woman would inform Shakespeare herself.

"I must also be going," White Eagle noted, rising. He stepped over to the infant first and spoke a few words in the Flathead language that made Wind In The Grass and Flower Woman smiled broadly, and then departed.

No sooner was the chief gone than Flower Woman

impulsively moved over to Wind In The Grass and tenderly stroked his cheek. "Do you see?," she signed. "Now you are accounted a true warrior. By tomorrow the whole village will know White Eagle paid us a visit. We will no longer be shunned by our own people."

"And we owe it all to Grizzly Killer," Wind In The Grass stated, affectionately placing his hand on Nate's arm.

Flower Woman gazed fondly at Nate. "I will feed you until you burst."

"Thank you," Nate signed. "But we should not overeat if we are riding out after the Blackfeet tonight."

"Oh. Yes. I did not think," Flower Woman commented sheepishly, and turned to the fire to begin her preparations.

Nate felt Wind In The Grass give him a squeeze, and then the warrior went over to Roaring Mountain. The sight of the family happily engaged in mundane activities prompted him to think yet again of Winona. He wondered what she was doing.

Many miles to the south, outside of a sturdy cabin overlooking a serene lake teeming with waterfowl and fish, stood a beautiful Indian woman in a beaded buckskin dress, her dark hair flowing down to her hips. She placed both hands on the mound that had once been her flat stomach and felt movement as the infant growing within kicked.

She smiled, at peace with herself. It would be a boy. She just knew it. And she would be the proudest woman alive when the child came forth into the world, proud because she had honored her husband in one of the highest ways any woman could honor the man she loved; by giving him the sacred gift of a new life, a child to carry on in the footsteps of the parents, to keep the family alive for generations to come.

Her mouth curling downward, she faced northward. Where are you, my husband? she mused. He had said that he would be back after two sleeps at the most. Did he decide to stay with his friend a while longer, perhaps to talk over whatever had been bothering him?

She knew he had been troubled, although he would not come right out and tell her the reason. She had not pried, not made a nuisance of herself by intruding on his private thoughts. Deep down, though, she worried, worried greatly.

What if he was losing interest in her?

The thought sparked intense terror. She often speculated on how much he missed his family back in New York City, wherever that was, and whether he felt any inclination to return to them. He'd tried several times to explain about the place where he had been born and spent most of his life, and once had even drawn a picture on a board with a piece of charcoal to show her how to get there. Even so, New York City seemed unreal to her, an alien place filled with strange people who lived incomprehensible lives, spending their days and nights devoted to the making of the strange paper and metal they worshipped above all else. According to her beloved, very few people in the entire city bothered to make a diligent effort to live in harmony with the Everywhere Spirit.

How could such a thing be? she had often asked herself. How could any people hope to flourish if they denied the source of all that existed? The stories he had told her seemed too incredible to be true, yet she knew he never lied. Stories about lodges made of stone, towering high in the air. Stories about mighty metal animals called steam engines that were expected to one day do the work of horses. And stories about people who were always on the go, from dawn to dusk, never giving themselves a moment's rest.

In a way, the white race reminded her of ants. As a young girl, she had spent many an idle hour observing an ant hill, watching the tiny creatures go about their lives, always in motion, always working, working, working, never taking time to enjoy the fruits of their labor.

Was it possible her husband missed such a distressing life? Did he secretly pine to go back? It would explain his unusual moody behavior of late. And she had to be honest; she knew of many Indian women who had taken white men as husbands, and in most of the cases the men had left the women after only a year or so to head east and never returned.

What if the same fate befell her?

She anxiously bit her lower lip and lightly smacked her right palm against her thigh. This was not the way for the wife of the mighty Grizzly Killer to act. She must not give in to her fear. To do so insulted him, insulted their love. He had been true to her from the first day they met, and in the depth of her soul she felt he would remain true until the day they died.

Turning, she walked toward the south end of the cabin where the pen holding their horses was situated. If she kept busy, she wouldn't have time for such foolish thoughts. She hummed, trying to cheer herself up, and rounded the corner.

The eight animals were idly munching on grass she had fed them earlier. A few gazed at her, then resumed eating.

Satisfied, she retraced her steps to the front door and just reached it when a tremendous commotion erupted at the lake. She pivoted, her eyes narrowing, seeking the source.

Every bird on the lake and in its immediate vicinity had taken wing. Ducks, geese, gulls, and others were flapping into the sky, voicing a chorus of distinct quacks and cries.

She saw nothing to account for the peculiar behavior, which worried her. There might be a predator abroad, perhaps a panther or a grizzly. If so, she couldn't afford to take any risks. She entered the cabin, then closed and locked the door. To the right, leaning against the wall, was a loaded flintlock. She patted the barrel, reassured by its feel, remembering the lessons her husband had given her in how to shoot the cumbersome gun and how pleased he'd been when one afternoon she'd consistently hit a circle he had carved in a tree from a distance of thirty yards. He had laughed and hugged her and kissed her until her lips had been sore.

Oh Nate, she wondered, where are you?

Chapter Fifteen

Nate opened his eyes to find Wind In The Grass shaking his left shoulder. He promptly sat up, yawned, and gazed at the entrance. The flap had been tied up, and through the opening could be seen part of the star filled heavens.

"It is time," Wind In The Grass signed.

"Did you get any sleep?" Nate asked.

"I tried," the young warrior said.

Placing a hand on the Hawken at his side, Nate rose. His mind felt sluggish, and he almost regretted taking the nap. He'd felt better several hours ago when he'd laid down on his blanket. But he'd needed the rest if he hoped to be fully alert once the hunt for the Blackfeet began. Turning, he saw Flower Woman at the back of the lodge, tenderly cradling Roaring Mountain in her arms, rocking the infant back and forth. "I should saddle my horse," he signed, and took his leave, giving Wind In The Grass time in private to say good-bye.

The cool air invigorated him as he stepped outside. His nostrils registered the sweet scent of burning wood, principally pine, and he inhaled deeply. Leaning his rifle against the lodge, he saddled the stallion. Then he double-checked to be certain all of his guns were loaded.

Wind In The Grass emerged, appearing rather downcast, and set about preparing his own horse.

"Is anything wrong?" Nate signed when the warrior glanced in his direction.

"Flower Woman is not very happy about my going."

"You can stay if you want," Nate suggested. "No one would hold it against you. Why risk your life when you have a young son and a wife to provide for?"

"You have a wife too," Wind In The Grass noted. "Yet I see you are all ready to go." He paused and sighed. "No, I gave my word, and I will accompany Carcajou and you."

Nate sympathized with the warrior's obvious inner turmoil since he felt the same way about having left Winona to help Shakespeare. Life sometimes required the making of hard decisions and compelled a man to do something he otherwise would never do, such as leaving one's family to venture into the jaws of danger. At such times the only thing a man could do was pray those jaws never snapped shut.

They both looked up as a white horse approached from the south.

"Well, look at you two eager beavers," Shakespeare declared in English, and chuckled as he halted near their mounts. "Are you ready to go?"

"I am," Nate said.

The mountain man addressed Wind In The Grass in the Flathead language, and the young warrior went into the lodge, stepping out a minute later with a parfleche in his left hand, a bow in his right.

"We'll head for Still Lake," Shakespeare told Nate. "If those vermin are still camped in the vicinity, we should be able to spot their campfire a long ways off. Then we'll sneak up on the devils and give them a taste of their own medicine."

"Suits me," Nate said, anxious to get underway. He wanted to bring up the subject of Blue Water Woman and ascertain his mentor's plans concerning Standing Bear. In a lithe motion he swung into the saddle and gripped the reins in his left hand, listening to Shakespeare explain their plan to Wind In The Grass.

The warrior was securing the parfleche to his stallion's back. He stopped to address McNair for a minute, then completed his work.

"What was that all about?" Nate inquired, using English.

"Wind In The Grass isn't too partial to the notion of fighting the Blackfeet when there are only three of us," Shakespeare translated. "And it's not that he's afraid. He's simply being practical and realistically weighing the odds."

"None of the Flatheads are too keen on tangling with the Blackfeet," Nate noted.

"Who can blame them? The Blackfeet have terrorized every tribe in the northern Rockies, the plains east of the mountains, and southern Canada for more years than most folks can recollect. They have more hunting territory under their control than any three tribes combined. As you well know, they're natural scrappers. They'll fight until they drop."

"I'm surprised they haven't conquered the entire Rocky Mountain region by now."

"If they ever take to the horse as heartily as most of the others tribes have, they will," Shakespeare predicted. "But they still insist on conducting their raids on foot, which limits their range and the speed of their attacks."

Wind In The Grass climbed onto his war stallion and signed, "I am ready, my friends."

Nate gazed up at the full moon as Shakespeare headed north, then fell in behind his mentor. And so it begins, he reflected, hoping the Blackfeet would be long gone when they arrived at the lake. The last thing he wanted was to tangle with those tenacious savages again. But as things now stood, he didn't have any choice.

Winona tensed, her hands frozen above the buckskins pants she had been sewing for Nate, her ears straining to catch another sound. She was positive she had heard a faint, guttural snarl, and waited for it to be repeated. Most likely it had been a prowling bobcat or a lynx, perhaps even a panther, which was little cause for alarm. None of the big cats ever came close to the cabin, undoubtedly because of the human scent.

Still, she worried about the horses. A panther, or even a lynx if it was starving, might decide to make one of the animals its next meal. And with her husband gone, the duty of protecting the animals fell on her shoulders. She listened for the horses to begin whinnying, a sure sign that something was lurking nearby, but there wasn't a peep out of them.

She resumed working on the pants, a present she would give Nate when he returned. If she kept herself busy, she had reasoned, she would be less prone to miss him and less likely to let her imagination run wild, conjuring up vivid images of all the sundry horrible fates that could befall her beloved. The heavy thread she was using, made from buffalo tendons, had to be unwound a bit further, so she lifted the stick that served as her spool and began slowly twirling it.

Just then, from the south, several of the horses neighed loudly.

She was out of the chair the next instant, scarcely

breathing as the animals continued to whinny. They were quite agitated and making a considerable racket. There was no doubt that something lurked outside. Placing the pants, the thread and the bone needle on the chair, she crossed silently to the window. A deerhide flap had been tacked over the opening for use in keeping out insects in the summer and the cold wind in the winter. Now she unfastened the bottom of the flap and rolled it up several inches, then bent at the waist and peered into the murky darkness beyond.

Something growled.

An involuntary chill rippled down her spine. She gripped the bottom sill so hard her knuckles turned white, then chided herself for losing control. Be calm, Winona, she told herself. It was just a wild animal, and she had seen countless wild animals during her life.

As with most women in her tribe, she had killed scores of rabbits, grouse, ducks, and other small game for her family's cooking pot. But the taking of larger game had been the sole province of the men. Only warriors were permitted to go on buffalo hunts or after deer and elk, and only warriors killed the occasional bear or panther. She hoped the creature out there wasn't one of the big predators.

Winona stared at the surrounding forest, trying to detect movement. All she saw were shadowy trees and gloomy undergrowth, nothing to give a hint of whatever it might be. Girding herself, she stepped to the door and picked up the flintlock.

All the horses were neighing now, creating a din that could be heard for half a mile.

She had to go out. There was a slim chance Utes might be camped in the area, and if they heard the horses they would be sure to investigate in the morning. She must quiet them immediately.

Holding the rifle firmly in her left hand, she opened

the door halfway and listened. From the commotion, the horses were milling around inside the pen in fearful confusion. She disliked the idea of stepping out there where the creature prowling about could see her better than she could see it.

An idea occurred to her, and she moved to the stone fireplace Nate's uncle had constructed when building the cabin. The fire crackled noisily, eating at the broken branches she had gathered earlier in the day. Taking hold of one end of a thick, short limb untouched by the flames, she carefully pulled it out and held the torch aloft. The light wouldn't last long, but perhaps it would scare off her unwanted visitor.

Feeling braver, Winona went straight outside, turned right, and stopped. She raised the torch as high as she could, scanning the vegetation, her heart beating wildly, ready to bolt inside should the creature turn out to be a huge grizzly.

One of the horses vented a particularly high-pitched whinny.

Figuring the prowler must be near the pen, Winona hastened to the end of the cabin, the flickering flames dancing as if alive and casting their glowing radiance out to a distance of about eight feet. She halted again, extending the torch toward the animals, and saw them moving in a nervous circle, packed together for mutual protection.

There was no sign of whatever skulked in the woods.

Suddenly all the horses stopped and swung to the south, their nostrils flaring, their ears pricked, their collective attention riveted on the thick brush.

Winona heard something moving, heard a twig snap and another feral growl, and her body was instantly transformed into a block of ice. She stood still, her lips parted, afraid to take a breath. A large bush off to her left moved as if shaken by an invisible hand. Gulping, she swung the torch toward it and the shaking ceased.

The thing uttered a fierce snarl.

She knew it must be watching her and backed up until her back touched the log wall. Now, if the creature attacked, it wouldn't be able to come at her from the rear. One handed, she pointed the heavy flintlock at the bush, wondering how she was going to fire and hold the torch at the same time.

The horses had quieted down, comforted by her presence. They were all gazing toward the same bush, completely motionless, standing as if sculpted from clay.

Winona held the torch out and slowly moved it back and forth. The circle of light barely went half the distance to the forest, not illuminating the bush at all, and she realized she must get closer if she hoped to identify the creature. She hesitated, though, thinking of the new life within her, of the consequences to the baby should she become gravely injured. Nate might come back to find them both dead.

But she couldn't just stand there.

She edged forward, taking little steps, the rifle barrel swaying with each pace. Using her thumb, she cocked the hammer to set the trigger. Moments later she saw something.

Eyes. A pair of close-set, beady eyes were reflecting the torch light, gleaming reddish against the backdrop of foliage, fixed balefully on her.

Winona stopped. The eyes were too small and too low to the ground to be those of a bear or a panther. Her mind raced as she attempted to deduce its identity. Could it be a bobcat? she wondered, and dismissed the idea because the eyes weren't the proper shape.

The animal moved, gliding a few feet to its right, never once taking its eyes off her, and halted.

She noticed it had an odd, flowing sort of gait, and a

vague memory blossomed at the back of her mind, convincing her she should know what it was. Not wanting to provoke it, she remained rooted to the spot, moving only the torch so she could keep track of the beast's red orbs.

Again the thing moved, a few cautious steps, and its eyes rose several inches as if it had elevated its head.

Relief seeped into Winona. The creature clearly wasn't more than two feet high at the front shoulders, and she was confident she could dispatch the animal with a single shot if it should attack. To her surprise, the thing appeared about to do just that by moving a few feet toward her and giving voice to a growl that would have done justice to an enraged grizzly.

She saw more of it now, observing a heavyset body held close to the ground, apparently dark brown in hue and covered with the densest of fur. There also seemed to be a rather short tail. Those beady eyes blazed at her without once blinking. The breeze briefly shifted then, and she smelled the faintest of foul odors.

Then she knew. Her fear resurfaced, stronger than before, as she cried out "No!" in Shoshone. Her voice had a surprising effect; the creature started, whirled, and ran into the woods, its passage marked by much crashing of the undergrowth.

Winona was safe for now, but she still felt weak at the knees. The thing she had encountered was far worse than any grizzly or panther, far deadlier than any other animal. Its voracious appetite and tenacity were legendary among all the tribes, and few were the warriors who had ever bested one in battle. Elusive, fearless, and the most powerful animal in existence for its size, the mere mention of its name inspired utter dread.

Such was the reputation of the wolverine.

Chapter Sixteen

The moon was well past its zenith when Shakespeare led them to the top of a hill and reined up. "This is as far as we go on horseback," he announced, first in English, then in the Flathead tongue.

Nate didn't need to ask why. Visible a quarter of a mile away, resembling a large, pale mirror, shimmering with reflected moonlight, was Still Lake. Dismounting, he tied the reins to a nearby tree and faced his companions.

Shakespeare was scanning the area around the water. "I don't see any campfires, but we'll play it safe anyway. Slow and quiet is the way we'll do this." He started forward.

Doing the same, Nate looked over his shoulder at their Flathead friend. Wind In The Grass had not uttered a word since departing the village. He imagined the warrior was thinking about Flower Woman and Roaring Mountain, troubled by the prospect of never seeing them again. And Nate couldn't blame him one bit.

They flitted down the hill like ghosts through a cemetery, their footfalls virtually silent as was the forest all around them.

Nate didn't like the quiet one bit. There should be animal sounds, he mused, the many snarls and growls and squeals that regularly arose from the wilderness during those hours when many of the predators were abroad. But there was nothing save the wind rustling in the trees to even hint at the existence of life in the inky realm. Oddly, the wolves and coyotes were also silent and had been for some time.

Shakespeare demonstrated an uncanny knack for seeing in the dark, leading them around thorny thickets, over logs, and around other obstacles with the agility and fluid motion of a twenty year old. Every now and then he paused to listen and sniff.

What did he think he would smell? Nate wondered, grinning. Sometimes his mentor displayed eccentric behavior he found almost comical. Maybe the reason could be attributed to Shakespeare having lived for so many years in the wild among the animals. Anyone who lived with wild creatures long enough, Nate reflected, might well take on some of their mannerisms after a while.

Several times Nate glanced to his rear to verify Wind In The Grass still followed. The Flathead was exceptionally stealthy, his moccasin covered feet flowing effortlessly over the ground, his head cocked, an arrow notched to his bow string.

Nate held himself bent at the waist, his finger caressing the Hawken's trigger, treading in Shakespeare's footsteps. The lake grew nearer by the minute, but there were still no campfires in evidence. Even if the Blackfeet had retired to their forts hours ago, there should still be enough smoldering embers to mark the locations of those fires. But a shroud of black covered the landscape.

Shakespeare stopped more frequently now, glancing right and left. Suddenly he pressed a hand over his nose and mouth and motioned for them to do the same.

Not understanding, Nate hesitated, and a moment later the awful stench hit him with the force of a physical blow, making him gag and almost stagger backwards. He clamped a hand over the lower part of his face, barely inhaling, and gazed past his mentor to behold the source of the revolting stench.

A rotting corpse lay a dozen feet away.

They went around it. Nate was unable to take his eyes from the grisly legacy of the battle. He guessed it had been a Flathead. Stripped of all clothes and weapons, the body had suffered a fate typical of those who fell during Indian warfare. Most of the hair was gone, taken by a Blackfoot no doubt. The face had been mutilated, the nose and lips sliced off and the eyes gouged out. Both arms had been chopped off at the elbows and the legs below the ankles. Animals had been at the flesh, tearing off strips of skin to get at the juicy meat underneath. The gory remains disgusted him, and he felt bile rise in his gorge. He swallowed hard, refusing to be sick.

As they continued, they encountered more bodies, all in similar ghastly condition. The Blackfeet had butchered the fallen Flatheads just as the Flatheads had previously butchered the fallen Utes.

By breathing shallowly, Nate was able to avoid inhaling most of the odor. Still, his stomach was queasy by the time they came to the tree line. Before them were the forts, dark and apparently empty. He crouched behind a tree and studied the structures.

Shakespeare came over and squatted, then gestured for Wind In The Grass to join them. "I'm fixing to swing around to the west and come up on the forts from the rear. The two of you sit tight until I give you a signal."

"I'll go with you," Nate proposed out of concern for his friend's safety.

"I need you to cover the entrances in case there is someone inside, which I doubt," Shakespeare whispered. He spoke to Wind In The Grass for half a minute, then hastened off, vanishing in the undergrowth.

Nate trained the Hawken on the forts and impatiently waited for the mountain man to reappear. A stray cloud passed in front of the moon, plunging the landscape into total gloom, and he could barely see the end of his barrel. He glanced at the cloud, trying to will it to go faster, fearful Shakespeare would be attacked and he wouldn't be able to help because he couldn't see targets to shoot. Thankfully, the cloud drifted eastward before too long.

Focusing on the forts, Nate was surprised to see McNair was already there, creeping from the forest like a stalking panther. He steadied the rifle and cocked the hammer.

Wind In The Grass took a stride forward, elevated the bow, and partially drew back the string.

Moving rapidly, Shakespeare entered the first structure. He promptly emerged and went to the second, then the third. Finally he came out and waved.

Glad the Blackfeet were gone, Nate rose and hurried over.

"The varmints have skedaddled," Shakespeare declared, sounding disappointed. "They must be well on their way back to their own country with all their booty."

"White Eagle will be glad to hear the news," Nate said, letting the hammer down. He lowered the rifle, turned, and stared out over the tranquil lake, feeling extremely fatigued, the nap not having refreshed him as much as he had hoped. Now they could return to the village and get some real rest. A pinpoint of flickering light in the distance, at the base of a mountain range approximately four miles off, arrested his attention. "What's that?" he asked, knowing the answer but hoping he was wrong.

His companions turned.

"It's a campfire," Shakespeare said.

Nate's elation immediately evaporated. "The Blackfeet, you reckon?"

"Maybe," Shakespeare replied. "Maybe other Indians. Or it could be white men, for all we know." He walked toward the forest. "There's only one way to find out."

Disappointment turned to resentment as Nate hastened to their horses. With each passing hour his conscience bothered him more and more. He wanted to return to Winona, and it angered him that yet another delay barred his departure. There was nothing to prevent him from simply riding homeward whenever he wished—except his devotion to Shakespeare, and he couldn't bring himself to desert his best friend—yet. But if things didn't come to a head soon, if the Blackfeet hadn't truly left and if Shakespeare didn't resolve his dispute with Standing Bear, he would be forced to make a most distasteful decision, to chose between his beloved wife and his mentor.

Winona came awake with a start and sat bolt upright in bed, her mind racing as she struggled to become fully alert. Something had awakened her, but what? She glanced around, listening intently.

All appeared to be in the order. A single charred log still glowed reddish-orange in the fireplace; otherwise, the interior was plunged in darkness. A faint breeze stirred the flap covering the window. Outside, silence ruled. Not even the horses were stirring.

So what could it have been?

She swung her legs around and touched her bare feet to the floor. The cool air from the window faintly fanned her left cheek while the heat from the fireplace warmed her right. Perhaps, she reasoned, a dream had been responsible for interrupting her slumber, although for the life of her she couldn't recall having dreamed anything since falling asleep.

Very unusual.

Winona grinned at her foolishness and went to lie back down. Then, from near the door, came a loud scratching noise repeated three times.

An animal was clawing at the cabin!

She knew who the culprit must be, and a paralysis sparked by sheer fear glued her to the bed. The loaded rifle was propped against the wall near the entrance, but it might as well be on the next mountain. She was simply too scared to go get it.

A growl broke the silence and the animal renewed its assault, its claws tearing into the wood with rhythmic precision as first one paw, and then the other, ripped in vertical strokes.

The wolverine had returned.

Taking a breath, Winona compelled her body to stand. Perhaps the glutton, as many called the beasts, had never left. Perhaps it had been lurking in the woods, waiting for her to go to sleep, for the lights to go out and quiet to descend, before approaching the cabin.

She took a few tentative steps toward the rifle. Staring at the front of the cabin, she realized the creature wasn't trying to claw its way through the wall; it was concentrating on the weaker door. How did it know to do that? she wondered. Then she figured it had observed her come inside earlier and its rudimentary brain had compared the open doorway to the open holes of the burrows of some of its victims.

Wolverines would eat anything they could find and slay. They were known to prefer carrion, but the most knowledgeable Shoshone hunters also claimed wolverines would eat birds, squirrels, badgers, and a host of smaller game. They had also been known to kill deer, elk, and moose bogged down in heavy snow. Hunters had witnessed encounters between wolverines and grizzlies in which the wolverines drove the mighty bears from their kills and claimed the carcasses as their own. Wolverines would even readily fight the big cats.

Winona was most worried about another aspect to wolverine lore. Many times wolverines had raided lodges or cabins temporarily vacated by their owners and consumed every edible morsel within while systematically destroying every possession. It seemed this particular wolverine entertained a similar intention.

What was she to do?

She girded herself and tiptoed to the rifle, watching the door tremble as the beast clawed at the bottom. Once her hands closed on the weapon she felt somewhat better. Moving back a few paces, she pointed the flintlock at the door.

The wolverine stopped clawing.

Had it heard her? Winona reflected. Loud sniffing ensued, arising from the narrow crack between the floor and the door. She took another step backward, aware it was trying to pick up her scent.

Voicing a growl that would have done justice to the largest grizzly that ever lived, the wolverine tore into the door with extra vigor.

Winona swallowed hard. The thing knew she was there, and her intuition told her the wolverine wasn't all that interested in the contents of the cabin. It wanted her.

The door shook violently now. Occasionally the tips of a few claws would jut under the bottom, trying to get a firm purchase.

Desperate to drive the beast off, Winona shouted as loud as she could in Shoshone. "Go away, destroyer! Leave this place in peace!"

The clawing ceased.

Winona waited, her body tingling in anxious anticipation, hoping the yell had driven the monster off. The time dragged by and nothing happened. Encouraged, she crept to the door and pressed her right ear to the upper half.

In an explosion of fury the wolverine attacked the door once more, its paws pumping in a frenzy, its lethal claws biting into the wood like ten slender tomahawks, slowly chopping the stout door to bits.

Caught off guard, Winona jumped backwards, her limbs quivering in fright. She closed her eyes, directing her concentration inward, striving to control her surging emotions. This was no way for a Shoshone woman to behave, she berated herself. Shoshone women were raised to be worthy of the men they married and to be a credit to their people. Her behavior so far had been almost cowardly, and it was time she lived up to the standards of her tribe and the teachings instilled in her from childhood by her mother, her grandmother, and other women who had lived to ripe years and knew the way of wisdom all women should follow.

Kneeling, Winona cocked the flintlock and placed the end of the barrel within a hand's width of the door, aligning it with where she felt the wolverine stood. For all she knew, she might miss or merely wound the beast, which would only increase its rage and place her life in graver jeopardy, but she had to try something before it got through the door. Once the wolverine broke inside, she would be easy prey.

She willed her arms to hold steady, glanced at shadowy claws that materialized under the door, took a breath as Nate had taught her, and squeezed the trigger.

Chapter Seventeen

Nate hauled on the reins and brought his stallion to a stop. He glanced around in confusion, bothered by an acute sensation of imminent danger, but all he saw was Stygian forest. The feeling intensified, filling him with inexplicable dread, and he raised the Hawken halfway to his shoulder in case it should be needed.

"What's wrong?" Shakespeare asked. He had halted a dozen feet ahead and was gazing back in perplexity.

"I'm not sure," Nate replied.

"Did you see something?"

"No."

"Did you hear something?"

"No."

"Did you *smell* something?"

"Of course not."

"Then why in the world are you all set to shoot anything that moves?" Shakespeare asked in exasperation.

"I don't rightly know," Nate admitted, unable to

find anything menacing them. "I have a strange feeling, is all."

"Oh?" Shakespeare said, and surveyed the woodland. "What kind of feeling?"

"I don't rightly know."

The mountain man made a puffing sound. "If anyone ever accuses you of being a fount of information, tell them they're off their rocker."

As suddenly as the strange feeling came over Nate, it dissipated. He slowly lowered the Hawken and commented, "I'm sorry. I just don't know what to make of it."

"Maybe it was supernatural," Shakespeare suggested with a straight face.

"You've been in the saddle too long," Nate responded. "All the bouncing up and down has addled your brain."

"There are more things in heaven and earth, Horatio, than are dreamt of in your philosophy," Shakespeare quoted, and then altered his voice to a crackling whine. "Double, double toil and trouble, fire burn and cauldron bubble."

"Is that supposed to mean you're quite serious?"

"Quite, and rather eloquently too, if I do say so myself," Shakespeare said, leaning toward him. "Do you still have the feeling?"

"No, it's gone."

"And so are we unless it should return," Shakespeare said, and continued toward their destination.

Picking up the reins, Nate rode onward. The campfire still blazed and was now less than half a mile distant, leading him to question the wisdom of drawing any closer on horseback. They were in thick forest, hemmed in by underbrush, causing their animals to make more noise than he believed prudent.

Several hundred yards farther on, Shakespeare

lifted his arm to signify they should rein up.

Nate gladly did so, then secured the stallion to a tree. He studied the campfire, which was now glowing dully as if burning itself out. With Shakespeare on his right and Wind In The Grass on his left, he advanced warily. As the distance narrowed, it became apparent the camp was situated at the base of a steep cliff, hidden among a cluster of enormous boulders. Through a narrow crack between two of them the fire could be seen.

He realized he'd been lucky in spotting it. Whoever was in there had gone to great lengths to conceal their presence. If not for some of the firelight reflecting off the boulders and intensifying the illumination, he would never have seen the campfire.

The forest ended seventy-five yards away, and a grassy stretch of open land spread out before them.

Shakespeare stopped at the tree line and squatted. "If they've posted a guard, we'll never make it across."

"Do we wait until daylight?" Nate asked.

"Might be our best bet," Shakespeare said.

Wind In The Grass spoke up, conversing with the mountain man at length. Then he placed his bow on the ground, unslung his quiver, and drew his knife. Easing to his hands and knees, he quickly crawled into the high grass and was swallowed by the darkness.

Nate almost reached out a hand to stop him, but he guessed where his host was going and knew there was nothing he could say that would change the warrior's mind. "Is he doing what I think he's doing?" he whispered.

"Yep. He volunteered to sneak over there and see who it is," Shakespeare said.

"What can we do?"

Shakespeare sank onto his buttocks and rested his

rifle across his thighs. "Sit here and twiddle our thumbs until he gets back."

If he gets back, Nate reflected.

At the booming discharge of the flintlock the wolverine emitted a tremendous, raspy snarl, and Winona heard it thrashing wildly about, its body smacking against the door over and over. She shoved to her feet and dashed to the table on which she had placed the ammunition pouch and powder horn Nate had given her. Reloading, due to her lack of proficiency, was a slow, meticulous process. She had to be careful not to put too much black powder into the rifle or she ran the risk of the barrel bursting. Breathing heavily from the excitement, she managed to complete the task and hurried to the door.

The thrashing and snarling had stopped.

She listened, but heard only the wind. Had she killed it? Squatting, she found the hole in the door made by the ball as it bored through the wood. She figured the beast was wounded at the very least, hopefully fatally. It might drag itself off to die, ending her problem.

Kneeling, Winona placed an eye to the hole and gazed out. She could see a narrow strip of ground in front of the door, and there was no sign of the wolverine. Which didn't mean all that much. The creature might be lurking nearby, waiting for her to emerge, craving vengeance.

She went to rise and grab the latch, then thought better of the idea. As long as she stayed in the cabin, she was safe. Once outside, she was in the wolverine's element. The beast's acute senses would give it a decided advantage over her, but only while night lingered. Once daylight arrived, she would be on an equal footing.

Moving to the right of the door, she sat down and

leaned her shoulder against the wall. She would wait until morning before venturing out. Perhaps the wolverine would be gone by then if it wasn't already dead.

Fatigued, she closed her eyes and felt the baby move, a tickling sensation that brought a smile to her sagging lips. The baby. Above all else she must not endanger the baby's life.

One of the horses neighed.

Winona's eyes snapped open and she straightened in consternation. If the beast went after their animals, she must protect them. Surely though, she hoped, a wounded wolverine would not risk entering a pen of terrified horses where it could be trampled to death if they went into a frenzy. But there was no predicting the behavior of such volatile beasts.

There were no other sounds from the pen.

She leaned against the wall again, relieved. Her thoughts drifted to Nate, and she prayed to the Everywhere Spirit that he would return soon. All would be well if only he would come home.

The great Grizzly Killer.

Winona grinned, thinking of how awkward he had been when first they met, afraid to touch her or kiss her, as if their romance had been so fragile it would shatter at the slightest expression of affection. She chuckled. Her darling husband had exhibited undeniable courage when battling the scourge of the Rockies, but he had also exhibited the timidity of a little rabbit during the early months of their acquaintance, which had made for a peculiar combination of personality traits. And he still hadn't completely overcome his awkwardness. In a way, she hoped he never did. There was a sparkling boyish quality about him she found appealing, a quality rarely found in grown Indian men who learned at an early age the cruel realities of life and matured accordingly. Perhaps Nate's background accounted for the difference. In any event, it hardly mattered. She loved him as he was.

Time passed.

Her eyelids drooped against her will and she found her mind tottering on the brink of sleep. Sweet sleep. She needed more rest recently than in days past, no doubt due to the baby. When Nate had broached the subject of visiting McNair, she'd almost protested because she knew she would not get as much sleep while he was gone. Dutifully, she'd suppressed the impulse and agreed going to see Shakespeare was a good idea. So, in a sense, she had only herself to blame for being alone now when she knew very well Nate would have stayed had she but voiced the slightest objection.

Love, she decided, made people do things they would never do otherwise. In the name of love they were more considerate, more tolerant, more compassionate. And more stubborn.

Winona's shoulders slumped as she drifted off, and her last thought before falling asleep was for her husband's safety.

"What's taking him so long?" Nate inquired, gazing at the boulders. The campfire had gone out an hour ago, plunging the base of the cliff into darkness.

"When sneaking up on Blackfeet, it's not very smart to advertise your presence," Shakespeare responded, his back propped against a tree. "Not unless you like the notion of going around bald the rest of your life."

"I know that."

"Then relax, Nate. Wind In The Grass knows what he's doing. He'll be back soon."

"Speaking of getting back, what are your plans once we return to the village?"

"To dazzle Blue Water Woman with my charm and handsome features, then get her drunk and trick her into marrying me."

Nate nearly laughed. "But she already wants you to be her man."

"I know," Shakespeare said. "If we were back in the civilized world, she'd be a prime candidate for admittance to one of those sanitariums."

"You're in an awfully good mood," Nate noted.

"Why shouldn't I be? One of the prettiest women alive wants to cuddle with my cold feet at night, which qualifies an old cuss like me as one of the luckiest men alive."

About to make a comment about Blue Water Woman's taste in men, Nate spied a vague figure rising out of the grass and brought his rifle to bear.

"It's Wind In The Grass," Shakespeare said.

The Flathead came up to them and sank to one knee, then addressed Shakespeare.

All Nate could do was listen in suspense while the pair discussed whatever the warrior had found. When, a minute later, there was a pause in the conversation, he looked at the mountain man and said, "Well?"

"There are four Blackfeet encamped at the bottom of that cliff, under a rock overhang. None of the four have horses, and none appeared to have any scalps. Wind In The Grass believes they stuck around because they failed to count coup during the battle and intend raiding the Flathead village. They probably came to this spot to camp because they felt the Flatheads might return to Still Lake in greater force."

"Just the four of them will tangle with the entire village?"

"It would be real easy for them to slip in at night, grab a few horses and maybe a woman or two, and light out before the Flatheads knew what hit them," Shakespeare explained.

"So what do we do?" Nate asked. "Sneak on in there and kill them while they sleep?"

"We could, but it wouldn't be the honorable thing to do."

"What, then?"

"We wait here until daybreak, and when they show their faces we stand up and challenge them to a fight."

"Just like that?" Nate said sarcastically. He would much rather shoot them and be done with it. Fighting for personal honor and glory was fine, but not when he had a pregnant wife many miles away who needed him at home.

"Unless you have a better way," Shakespeare said.

"No," Nate confessed.

"If you'd rather sit this out, we'll understand," Shakespeare remarked.

"Count me in," Nate said, and moved over to the next tree. He propped the Hawken against the bole, then sat with his forearms draped over his bent knees. Melancholy set in, and he found himself feeling sorry he had ever set off after McNair. All he could think of was Winona, in the cabin alone, easy prey for any wild animal that might catch her outside or any hostile Indians who stumbled on their remote valley.

Days ago, when he'd found Shakespeare's cabin in such disarray, his obligation to his friend had seemed so clear-cut, so absolute. Now, he perceived he'd made a major mistake. He should have gone home to his wife. By virtue of having taken him as her mate for the rest of her born days, she deserved his unstinting devotion.

Loyalty to friends was all well and good, but when he got down to the crux of the matter, to the morality of his act, he now knew with granite certainty that a husband should always—*always*—be loyal first and foremost to his wife. All other obligations were secondary.

Nate gazed at the myriad stars sparkling in the firmament and imagined Winona snug in their bed, sleeping peacefully, as safe as could be. He hoped.

Chapter Eighteen

The screech of a jay brought Winona out of her slumber. She sat up, saw the sunlight streaming in the gap below the window flap, and beamed. Daylight. Now she could check on her nocturnal visitor. Rising, she almost toppled over before discovering both of her legs had also fallen asleep during the night. She leaned on the wall for support, feeling a tingling sensation in both limbs, then shook them to fully restore the circulation.

Once satisfied her legs were back to normal, she gripped the rifle and cautiously opened the door a crack. The bright light made her blink, compelling her to wait until she could see clearly before pulling the door all the way open and stepping into the brisk morning air.

She saw the blood right away, a large dark crimson puddle to the left of the doorway, congealed into an irregular mass from which a few blades of brown grass protruded. So she had hit the beast! She scanned the ground in front of the cabin but saw neither the wolverine nor any more patches of blood.

Encouraged, confident the animal was somewhere off in the brush dying in private as most animals preferred to do, Winona moved to the south and stared at the horse pen. The animals were fine, standing at ease, a few nibbling on bits of feed left over from yesterday.

The danger had passed.

In the brilliant sunshine her fears of the night before seemed childish, more the result of the stress she was under and an overactive imagination than any threat the wolverine had posed. Why had she let herself become so distraught when the beast could never get inside to harm her?

Winona laughed, spun on her heels, and walked back into the cabin to begin her daily routine. Now if only her husband would get back, everything would be perfect.

On the way inside she paused to stare once more at the puddle. The amount of blood convinced her the wolverine was most certainly dead or very close to it.

Most certainly.

Nate didn't sleep all night. As the sun crowned the eastern horizon he took hold of the Hawken and stood. Shakespeare and Wind In The Grass were already on their feet and advancing into the field. He moved between them and lightly touched the stock to his shoulder.

"Wind In The Grass wants to be the one to challenge them," Shakespeare said. "We'll follow his lead."

Nate nodded. If the young warrior could count coup and take scalps, particularly Blackfeet scalps, it would elevate his status as a warrior immeasurably. The

Flathead had proven his courage and reliability by bringing the horses during the battle at the lake; now, Wind In The Grass would go one step farther, would join the ranks of those privileged warriors who had counted coup on their most dreaded enemies. Either that, or he would die trying.

They advanced twenty yards, spreading out, their weapons ready.

Nate scanned the huge boulders, his thumb glued to the hammer. Suddenly he saw movement and halted. Four buckskin clad warriors walked into view, all young, all armed with bows and knives and tomahawks, all conversing animatedly, perhaps about their plans for raiding the village.

The tallest of the Blackfeet gazed out over the grassy tract and halted, barking words to his fellow warriors. Every one stopped, their features betraying their astonishment. Arrows were hastily yanked from quivers.

Wind In The Grass walked ten more feet. He hefted his bow and hailed them in a mocking tone.

"What's he saying?" Nate asked.

Shakespeare snorted. "He's telling them he wants to learn whether the Blackfeet are as brave as everyone says, or whether they are all cowards who only attack from ambush or fight women and children."

The tall Blackfoot shouted a reply.

"He just told Wind In The Grass his mother was suckled by a mongrel and his father was afraid of his own shadow," Shakespeare translated.

At a gesture from the tall warrior, the Blackfeet started toward them.

"When will they get to fighting?" Nate asked, every nerve on edge, wishing they would conclude the fight instead of wasting time by shouting insults back and forth.

"Be patient," Shakespeare said. "Indians aren't always in a godforsaken rush like most white men. They take their time and do things right. After the challenges are out of the way, you'll have all the bloodshed you can handle."

Wind In The Grass and the tall Blackfoot exchanged further insults. All the while, the four Blackfeet came nearer and nearer, negating any range advantage the two Hawkens possessed.

Nate cocked his rifle, his palms feeling clammy, sweat breaking out on his brow. He concentrated on the warrior directly across from him, watching the man's hands. To his rear a loud fluttering and chirping occurred as a flock of birds took panicky wing from the forest. He thought little of it. Maybe an animal had spooked them, he reasoned.

Suddenly Wind In The Grass vented a fluttering shriek, his personal war cry, and whipped his bow up.

The Blackfeet reacted instantly, elevating their own bows.

At last! Nate took a bead on his target, held the barrel rigid, and fired, the Hawken blasting and bucking in his hands. The warrior had his bow string all the way back when the ball took him in the mouth, twirled him around where he stood, and dropped him in a heap.

Then everything happened incredibly fast. Nate glimpsed three shafts streaking toward them, heard Shakespeare's rifle crack and saw a second Blackfoot fall, and pivoted to avoid the shaft whizzing at his chest. To his amazement, another arrow flashed out of nowhere first, narrowly missing his torso. It came from behind them!

The arrow fired by the Blackfoot flew past a fraction of a second later and Nate glanced at the tree line, not knowing what to expect but certainly not expecting to find Standing Bear and Bad Face, each nocking arrows to their bow strings. In a rush of insight he realized the awful truth. The duo had trailed them from the village and had chosen this most vulnerable of moments to strike, while their backs were turned and they were preoccupied, to eliminate Standing Bear's rival and achieve their vengeance for the insults Nate had handed them. Conveniently, the deaths would be attributed to the Blackfeet. "Shakespeare! Wind In The Grass!" he bellowed, aware the Flathead wouldn't be able to understand but hoping Wind In The Grass would look anyway. "Behind us!"

He began reloading, trying to look every which way at once, appalled by the sight in each direction. One of the Blackfeet was still alive and charging toward them. Shakespeare had seen Standing Bear and Bad Face and was frantically feeding black powder into his rifle. And as he glanced at Wind In The Grass, the young warrior was hit squarely between the shoulder blades by an arrow from the rear.

Nate dropped to his knees, giving his adversaries less of a profile to aim at, and crammed a ball and patch into the rifle. Looking up, he saw his newfound friend pitch into the grass. The Blackfoot was coming on strong, another shaft ready to fly. So were Standing Bear and Bad Face.

Shakespeare's Hawken spoke, and Standing Bear's malevolent face developed a new hole in the center of the forehead. The Flathead tripped over his own feet and toppled.

Leaving two foes, Bad Face and the sole remaining Blackfoot.

Nate raised his rifle, about to fire when Shakespeare cried out in pain and he shifted to see his mentor going down, an arrow sticking from the grizzled mountain man's chest.

Shakespeare!

Livid rage brought Nate to his feet, whirling as he stood, the Hawken tucked tight to his right shoulder. The bead settled on the Blackfoot's head and he squeezed off the shot. Not even bothering to verify the result, he whirled again, letting go of the Hawken to claw at both flintlocks, the patter of Bad Face's moccasins in his ears.

The hateful Flathead was eight yards away, an arrow drawn back to his cheek, grinning in triumph.

Nate was a blur. He extended and cocked the pistols, his blood boiling as he fired both at the same instant Bad Face loosed the shaft. His twin balls cored the Flathead's chest, lifting Bad Face from his feet and hurling him to the ground. Nate felt something tug at his hair, and then the fight was over as abruptly as it had begun. He was the only one standing, shrouded by acrid gunsmoke.

For a moment he stood there, dazed by the savagery and the toll. He thought of Shakespeare and turned, shocked to discover the mountain man sitting up and glaring at the arrow in his body. "Shakespeare!" he cried, running over. "How bad is it?"

"It tickles like hell."

"Tickles?" Nate repeated in disbelief.

Shakespeare nodded and twisted to afford a clear view. The arrow had actually struck him on the right side of his chest, penetrating at an angle through the flesh covering the ribs. The barbed point, coated with blood, protruded four or five inches from the back of his buckskin shirt, about level with his shoulder blade. "Give me a hand," he said, gripping the feathered end of the shaft with both hands.

"What do you want me to do?" Nate asked.

"We can't leave this in," Shakespeare said, his features flushed. Unexpectedly, he tensed and exerted pressure on the arrow, snapping it off close to his body, gritting his teeth to keep from calling out. The effort weakened him and he sagged.

"You should have let me do that," Nate chided him, tucking the pistols under his belt. He squatted and placed a hand on Shakespeare's shoulder.

"Pull out the other half," the mountain man directed.

"Now?"

"We could wait for spring, but I might not last that long," Shakespeare said, mustering a grin. "Do it, please. The sooner it's out, the sooner we can clean and cauterize the hole."

Frowning distastefully, Nate moved behind him and gingerly grasped the arrow below the point, the blood coating his palms. He feared his hands would be too slippery to maintain a firm purchase, but when he gave the shaft a sharp wrench, it slid right out.

Shakespeare gasped and arched his back, then exhaled loudly and said, "Thanks. You'd better check on Wind In The Grass and the bastards we fought before we finish up with me."

"Be right back," Nate promised, and sprinted toward their Flathead friend, dreading what he would find.

The arrow had transfixed Wind In The Grass from back to front, evidently puncturing the heart. A pool of blood rimmed the warrior's body, spreading outward. His eyes were open, lifelessly fixed on the grass that had been his namesake.

Profound sadness formed a lump in Nate's throat. Why had Standing Bear and Bad Face gone after Wind In The Grass? he wondered, and reached an obvious conclusion; they hadn't wanted any witnesses. He thought of Flower Woman and Roaring Mountain and tears moistened his eyes.

Not now! he chided himself, gazing out over the field at the bodies dotting the ground. He must make certain all of their enemies were dead. Quickly reloading the flintlocks, he went from corpse to corpse. Not a flicker of life among them.

"Wind In The Grass?" Shakespeare inquired as he walked back.

Nate simply shook his head.

"Damn. That's a shame," Shakespeare said morosely, his hand pressed over the blood stain on his shirt.

"What will happen to his wife and son?"

"Flower Woman is a fine woman. Most likely another warrior will take her into his lodge and raise the boy as his own. Don't worry. Indian women are tough. They know all about making do."

Making do? Yes, maybe that was the best way to describe the life of someone who had lost the person they loved most in all creation. Nate headed for the woods. "Don't move. I'll have a fire started in no time."

He set about collecting broken limbs, preoccupied with thoughts of life and death, love and emptiness, happiness and sorrow, and Winona. Of all the worst possible fates that could befall him, being deprived of her company for the rest of his life would be the ultimate injustice. She had become as much a part of him as the air he breathed and the water he drank. Her love was more priceless than all the gold ever mined and the most expensive diamonds ever produced.

Unbidden, memories of New York filled his mind. He recalled married friends who had often neglected their wives and families to go off with their chums, carousing or gambling to all hours. Back then, he'd admired their independence and laughed at their antics. Now, he saw them for what they had been.

Soon he had enough limbs and hastened to Shakespeare's side. "How are you holding up?"

The mountain man was sitting quietly, staring at a distant majestic mountain. "Just fine. How about you?"

"Me? I wasn't hit," Nate said, depositing the branches at his feet.

"No, but I saw the look on your face a while ago. Were you thinking about Winona?"

Nate glanced at him in surprise. "Do you read thoughts now?"

Shakespeare shook his head. "I would be thinking of her if I was in your shoes. As soon as I'm patched up, head for home."

"First I'll drop you off at the village," Nate said. "Blue Water Woman should have you as fit as a fiddle in no time. Bring her for a visit when you can. I'm sure Winona will be delighted to have the company."

"I bet she will," Shakespeare agreed. "The poor woman must be bored to death sitting around that cabin with nothing to do but talk to you."

Chapter Nineteen

Her husband was on his way home!

Winona stood on the west shore of the lake, an empty bucket in her left hand, and gazed northward. She couldn't explain exactly how she knew, but she knew. In her bones she felt she would soon be holding her man in her arms once again, and she was ecstatic. The baby reacted to her joy by giving her a good, solid kick.

She knelt at the water's edge and dipped in the bucket. Since the incident with the wolverine two days ago, the tranquility of her life at their humble cabin had been undisturbed. She had finished sewing the pants for Nate and was trying to decide what to make him next. A new hat would be nice. The one he occasionally wore had been taken from a dead Blackfoot warrior named Mad Dog, the same warrior who was directly responsible for the deaths of her mother and father. She disliked seeing it on her husband's head; it brought back too many acutely painful memories. If she made him a new one, they could get rid of Mad Dog's.

Nate had caught hundreds of beaver during the last trapping season, and the pelts were now safely cached out behind the cabin. He intended to take them to the next rendezvous and sell them for the highest dollar they could command, but she knew he wouldn't mind if she took a few to make the hat.

Using both hands, she lifted the almost full bucket from the cold lake and stood. Nearby floated a flock of ducks, eyeing her hungrily. Sometimes she brought them food and they would gather within an arm's length of her legs to quack incessantly in the hope of getting a morsel. "Not today, little ones," she told them, grinning, and headed for the cabin.

Soon darkness would descend. Half of the sun had already disappeared, and the lengthening shadows of early evening were spreading out over more and more ground, shrouding the undergrowth in gloom.

Winona hummed as she retraced her steps. The horses had been fed, the cabin cleaned, and she had a fresh supply of water to last through the night. She looked forward to relaxing and getting a good night's sleep.

Once inside she locked the door, placed the bucket on the table, and went to the window. A little air would be delightful, she reasoned, and rolled the flap all the way up, securing it with the strips of rawhide tacked to the top.

She busied herself making supper, boiling a grouse she had killed with an accurately aimed stone that very morning. After pouring more water into the big pot above the fire, she stirred the meat and herbs she had mixed together before going to the lake. The tantalizing aroma made her mouth water.

Winona pulled the chair closer to the fireplace and

took a seat, glad to be off her feet. Her stamina wasn't what it used to be, a condition that would remedy itself after the baby was born. She placed her hands on her tummy, waiting for the infant to squirm, and closed her eyes. Lassitude pervaded her body. The soft crackling of the fire, the light bubbling of the water, and the faint breeze stroking her hair lulled her into dreamland.

Moments later she opened her eyes. Or so she believed until she noticed the fire had diminished considerably. Even so, the room was much darker than it should be during daylight hours. Twisting, she gazed out the window and was startled to see night had claimed the land while she slept. How long had she been out?

She rose and inspected the cooking pot. Half of the water in it had evaporated, indicating she had been asleep for hours. Chuckling, she went to the door and reached for the latch. An armful of branches would have the fire roaring again in no time.

From the horse pen there suddenly arose a series of frightened whinnies as first one animal, then another, expressed building fear.

Winona hesitated, her intuition blaring a warning in her brain. "It can not be," she said softly, and then felt her blood become icy as a chilling, all too familiar snarl came from outside.

The wolverine was back.

She scooped the flintlock into her hands and backed up a few paces. Some creatures, it seemed, were too persistent for their own good. Once it began tearing at the door, she'd fire another ball into its stocky body. This time, perhaps, she would end the threat once and for all.

Seconds later the wolverine obliged her by slashing at the door in a frenzy, growling the whole time. The door trembled but held.

Winona inched closer. She knelt and lowered her right eye to the hole made by the ball the other night. Through it she glimpsed the animal's furry form in perpetual motion as its claws raked deep grooves in the wood.

The wolverine stopped. She could see a shoulder—or was it a leg?—until the beast shifted position. One of its beady eyes appeared at the other end of the hole, balefully regarding her, and she recoiled in surprise.

Snarling, the wolverine renewed its attempt to get inside.

She leveled the rifle, holding the barrel at the height she estimated the beast's head would be, and braced herself to fire. From the din the wolverine created, it sounded as if the door was being reduced to kindling. If she didn't shoot soon, the bloodthirsty killer might get inside.

Winona fired, putting a hole inches to the left of the previous one. The blast hurt her ears, the pungent gunsmoke stung her eyes and nostrils. On its heels came absolute quiet as both the wolverine and the horses fell silent. She pushed to her feet and moved toward the table to reload.

Had she done it? Was the beast dead?

She picked up the powder horn, her eyes on the door, unable to detect any movement beyond. Out of the corner of her left eye, however, she did register motion and heard a thud. She pivoted to find the source and nearly dropped the powder horn as consternation gripped her soul.

Framed in the window, its shoulders partly through, its front legs dangling over the sill, was the living embodiment of primal ferocity. Exercising agility that rivaled a mountain lion's, the wolverine had leaped to the window and was now clinging fast. The moment she saw it, the beast growled and began pumping its rear legs to get a firmer purchase so it could push inside.

Winona knew she must stop it at all costs. If she could knock it off the sill and fasten the flap, she'd gain the time she needed to reload the flintlock. Placing the powder horn on the table, she dashed toward the window, firming her hold on the rifle and lifting it overhead to use as a club.

The wolverine went into a frenzy, snapping and snarling as it eased its body higher, close to gaining entry.

In three strides Winona was there and driving the rifle's stock into the beast's forehead. The wolverine recoiled but didn't lose its grip. She smashed it again, narrowly missing having her forearms torn open.

More of the glutton squeezed inside.

No! Winona mentally shrieked, and swung the rifle overhand like a club, the stock crunching into the wolverine's face. Blood sprayed from above its right eye, but it never flagged. If anything, its rear legs worked harder.

She realized the skull was simply too thick to damage and ran to the table. Another shot was her only hope. She started reloading, glancing countless times at the window as her fingers flew.

The wolverine had half of its body over the sill and was striving to get a purchase with its rear legs. Blood seeped from the gash above its eye and saliva dribbled from its open mouth. Its tapered teeth glistened in the firelight.

Winona fed the powder into the flintlock and went to put in the ball and patch. The futility of her act hit home. In moments the thing would be inside, well before she could get the gun loaded, and she would be completely at its mercy. She spun, casting about for something to use as a weapon. On a peg above the bed hung her knife, but she would have to cross the room to reach it and by then the wolverine would gain entry. Much closer was the fireplace.

In desperation she tossed the flintlock onto the table and dashed over, stooping so she could grab the unlit end of a burning branch and yank it from the fire. She whirled, horrified to see the wolverine's haunches were almost through. Holding the firebrand out from her body, she charged.

The wolverine, intent on the floor below as it went to jump, looked up upon hearing her footfalls.

Winona voiced an inarticulate cry of rage and rammed the firebrand into its left eye, the flames searing the orb and scorching the hair on contact. Hissing, the wolverine recoiled, and she promptly speared the firebrand into the other eye. The smell of burning flesh filled the air.

With a violent jerk of its hips, the wolverine tore loose of the window and dropped to the floor. Its vision blurred by the searing flames, it tried to focus while snarling its defiance and swinging its front paws.

Winona barely jumped back in time. The wolverine somehow pinpointed her position and closed in, snapping at her legs. Again she evaded those razor teeth, but in doing so she tripped and fell onto her back directly in its path. The impact jarred her body, making the baby kick.

The baby!

She grit her teeth, determined to defend the infant with her last breath, and scrambled to her knees. The wolverine opened its mouth wide and sprang. In a sheer reflex action, she drove the firebrand into the beast's mouth, driving the branch in as far as it would go, and then frantically threw herself to the rear to avoid the wolverine's claws.

The glutton went berserk, thrashing and spinning as it tried to pry the branch from its mouth, its claws unable to get a grip. Blood cascaded over its lips.

Gagging and sputtering, the wolverine smacked into the wall and halted, its side heaving, shaking its head vigorously.

Winona was afraid it would attack again. While it wouldn't be able to bite her, those wicked claws could tear her to ribbons. She backed up until she bumped into something, and glancing over her shoulder she saw the chair she had sat in. Pivoting, she grabbed the arms, then faced the wheezing predator, just as the wolverine mustered its strength and bounded across the floor toward her. She swung the chair with all her might at the very instant the beast sprang.

The big black stallion was flecked with sweat when Nate reached the top of a rise to the north of his cabin and broke into a broad smile. Home, at last! He'd ridden like a madman to reach Winona, pushing the stallion to its limits, and in ten minutes he would be hugging her tight.

He goaded the stallion down the rise, and once he hit level ground broke into a gallop again. No smoke wafted from the chimney, which struck him as odd. Normally, Winona liked to keep a fire going on chilly days and the February thaw was about over. The temperature last night had dipped into the low twenties, at least, and not warmed much during the day.

Anxiety gnawed at his mind like a beaver on a tree, bringing all of his worries to the forefront. What if something had happened to her? he speculated, and felt a twinge of terror.

Please, no.

He threaded among the trees at a rash speed, angling at the front of the cabin, and he was still a couple of dozen yards off when he noticed the door didn't seem quite right. It took him a few seconds to realize the reason, and when he saw the distinct claw marks and the deep grooves in the wood he felt lightheaded.

Something had tried to get in.

The stallion was still in motion when Nate vaulted out of the saddle, the Hawken clenched in his right hand, and sprinted madly to the door. He hesitated when his fingers touched the latch, fearful of what he might find within. Swallowing hard, he threw the door wide and leaped inside.

All appeared in order, but the cabin was empty. The bed had been made, the chairs neatly arranged around the table, and leaning against the wall was her flint-lock.

Where was *she?*

Confused, he took a step, then heard light laughter to his rear.

"Welcome home, husband."

Nate spun, rejoicing at the sight of his beloved standing in the doorway, her eyes aglow with affection, an impish grin creasing her full lips, her hands held behind her back. He reached her in two long strides and swept her into his arms, choked with emotion at their reunion. "Winona," he said breathlessly.

"It is nice of you to remember my name," she responded playfully. "You were gone so long, I thought you might have forgotten."

"Never," Nate stated, and tenderly kissed her. "I never stopped thinking about you for a minute."

"How is Shakespeare?" Winona asked, trying to maintain a casual conversation with moisture rimming her eyes and her voice quavering.

"He's taking a Flathead woman as his wife," Nate disclosed, "just as soon as he mends. A Blackfoot arrow caught him in the side."

"You fought the Blackfeet?"

"A couple of times," Nate said. "I'll tell you all about it later." He nodded at the door. "First tell me what happened here. Why is that door in the shape it's in?"

Winona grinned. "Mice."

"Be serious."

"Big mice."

"Why won't you tell me?" Nate inquired. "What are you trying to hide?"

"Nothing," Winona said. "But I know you. I know how upset you can become over things. I will tell you after you have had a chance to rest and eat."

Knowing better than to buck her when she had made her mind up, Nate sighed and touched her belly. "How is our baby?"

"Fine. He kicks all the time now."

Nate beamed. "I can hardly wait."

"Me too," Winona said, and gave him an ardent kiss that lingered on and on. At last she drew her head back and said, "I have a surprise for you."

"What kind of surprise?"

"A gift."

"When do I get it?"

In response, Winona brought her hands from behind her back and held out the hat she had worked on every waking moment since the chair had saved her life. "Here."

"Well, I'll be," Nate said, delighted. He leaned the Hawken against the wall and took her present, running his fingers through the soft, dark brown fur. "You've done a marvelous job," he complimented her, wishing he'd had the foresight to bring her something.

Winona brightened. "Thank you. I worked very hard to make it the best hat I have ever made."

"It's not beaver," Nate commented, examining the

fur carefully, his brow creasing in contemplation. "In fact, it's not like any other fur I've seen close up. What exactly is this made of?"

"Carcajou."

"Carca—," Nate began, and glanced down at the door. He blanched, his mouth going slack, and then embraced her. For the longest time they simply stood there, cheek to cheek, each aware of the other's heart pounding rapidly, oblivious to the world around them. He finally broke the silence by saying, ever so softly, "Never again."